THE VERY FIRST DOG

Book Three of the Sam and Gunny K9 Adventure Series

Joe Jennings

Karen,
From a fellow
author and contest
finalist.
Joe & Gunny

Joe Jennings
Visit my website at www.ghostsofiwojima.com

Printed in the United States of America

First Printing: Feb 2019
Amazon

ISBN- 9781791950033

DEDICATION

To all the of K9 Search and Rescue handlers. You may not have the very first dogs, but you've got some of the best.

Now this is the Law of the Jungle
as old and as true as the sky;
And the Wolf that shall keep it may prosper,
but the Wolf that shall break it must die.
As the creeper that girdles the tree-trunk
the Law runneth forward and back
For the strength of the Pack is the Wolf,
and the strength of the Wolf is the Pack.
—"THE LAW OF THE JUNGLE" BY RUDYARD KIPLING

CONTENTS

ACKNOWLEDGMENTS

THEY SAY, "IT TAKES A VILLAGE TO …..," well, to do just about anything. Once again, my village has come through for me with encouragement and some amazingly detailed error checking. Thanks again to Bonnie, Nan, Mac, Erika, Katie, Christian, the grandkids, and, as always, Betsy.

Special thanks to our friend, the actor David Chandler, for invaluable suggestions on plot and character, and to my new friend, Karen Berggren, for her professional proofing and editing.

Finally, thanks to the one without whose inspiration none of these books would have been written.

Good boy, Gunny.

AUTHOR'S NOTES

Those of you who have read the first two books in this series, *Ghosts of Iwo Jima* and *Ghosts of the Buffalo Wheel*, may find *The Very First Dog* a bit different. Gunny, Sam, and Rebecca are back, of course, but Steve, Luke, Iwo, Alicia, and others are taking some time off. Sees Wolf is back, and there is a new cast of characters that I hope you come to like

If you haven't read the first two books, don't worry. You can read *The Very First Dog* as a stand-alone story, and I've provided some background to help you put this tale in context with the others.

I've written this book so that it should be accessible to younger readers. That doesn't mean that I have changed the writing style or dumbed-down the vocabulary, it just means that this story doesn't require some of the violence, language, and other adult themes that were necessary parts of the first two books.

I've included something new for me — some pictures. A large part of this story concerns the animals of the Upper Pleistocene era, and I thought you'd like to see what some of these creatures looked like

As always, I hope that you enjoy reading *The Very First Dog* as much as I enjoyed writing it.

Joe Jennings
Eden, Utah
February, 2019

ANIMALS OF THE VERY FIRST DOG

MUCH OF THE STORY OF *THE VERY FIRST DOG* is set in what is now northern Europe about fifteen thousand years ago shortly after the glaciers of the current Ice Age had reached their maximum and begun to recede. Paleontologists refer to this as the Upper Pleistocene Era.

There are many animals in this book. Some will be familiar, others less so. The images on the following pages are here to give you a feel for the main characters in this story.

The last picture is one that I have included by popular demand.

The first image is a scene by Mauricio Anton showing animals of the Upper Pleistocene Era in Europe. From left to right: early horses, wooly mammoths, cave lions on a reindeer, and a wooly rhinoceros.

A painting by Heinrich Harder showing a pack of wolves attacking an auroch.

A cave lion by Heinrich Harder

A pair of Beringian wolves shown in a diorama at the Yukon-Beringia Interpretive Center. The wolves in *The Very First Dog* would have looked very much like these two.

A depiction by Apokritaros on Wikipedia of Megaloceros, the family of deer living in the Upper Pleistocene.

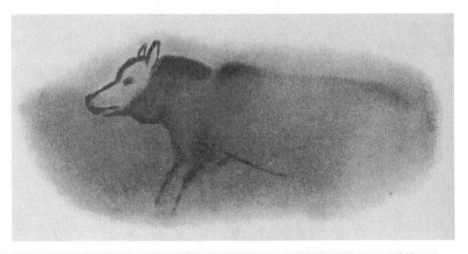

A tracing made by archaeologist Henri Breuil from a cave painting of a wolf-like canid, Font-de-Gaume, France dated 19,000 years ago.

The real Gunny. A photograph by Christian Peay

PROLOGUE

ONCE UPON A TIME — about fifteen-thousand years ago — there were no dogs.

There were dog-like creatures; jackals, coyotes, foxes, and, of course, wolves. For the previous twenty-thousand years or so, some of these canids had formed temporary alliances with our ancestors, the early *Homo sapiens*, but we have no evidence that any of these alliances lasted long enough to cause any significant change in the evolution of either the humans or the canids.

Up to the point where our story begins, our species had done pretty well for itself. We had outlasted the Neanderthals and the Denisovans and all of the other sub-species of *Homo*, and we had learned how to prosper in our world.

Then things began to change. The climate grew warmer, and the great ice sheets began to recede. The weather, the landscape, the flora and fauna all began to change. Some species evolved and grew. Others failed to adapt and died out. It wasn't at all clear what was going to happen to us.

The struggle for resources, especially food, became more intense every day, and it didn't seem that our species was very well equipped to compete. We were smart, we had tools and fire, but the other predators were faster, stronger, more powerful, and they had big teeth.

Fifteen-thousand years ago, when a band of humans went out to hunt, they were just as likely to end up being the prey as they were the predator. Their weapons allowed them to kill or snare many kinds of animals but were almost useless against a seven-hundred-pound cave lion or most of the other carnivores.

The human race was at a critical point in its history. To survive, to evolve, to become us, our ancestors needed something more. They needed a partner.

This is a story about how we found our partner.

CHAPTER ONE

Oldest Boy

HE WAS THE OLDEST BOY OF THE PEOPLE, so his name was Oldest Boy. Later, when he learned how he would serve The People, he would get his adult name. He hoped his new name would be something like Hunter or Scout, but it might be Tool Maker or Cooker. It depended on what he could do best to help The People.

The People lived in a small village of huts made from tree branches with roofs made from tightly woven strands of grass. The village sat at the base of a rocky ridge that marked the dividing line between the open grasslands that swept toward the Place Where the Sun Comes Up and the forest that seemed to go on all the way to the Place Where the Sun Goes at Night.

The rocky hill above the village provided a number of caves that were used for cooking and storing food as well as shelter when it was cold, or the weather was bad. Some of The People lived in caves all the time.

There was a large fire pit at the center of the village that was used when all of The People gathered together. There were smaller firepits at each hut and in most of the caves.

Memory was the story keeper, and her task was to keep all of the stories in her head so The People would never forget who they were and where they came from. Memory was old, but she was training one of the younger boys to be Memory when she was gone, so Oldest Boy didn't think he would be Memory.

Memory also had to count The People. When a new baby was born, or someone died, all of The People would come and stand very still around the firepit while Memory counted them. When Memory counted, she would hold up all of the fingers of both hands. When she touched a person, she would fold down one finger, and that person would leave. When she had folded down all her fingers, she would put a small rock in a bag on her belt. Then she would start again with all her fingers up. The last time she had counted The People she had put as many rocks as there are fingers on one hand plus one more rock into her bag. She had also put in as many pebbles as there are middle fingers. There were more People now than there had ever been before.

It was important to The People to know all these things, so Memory was a cherished member of The People.

There were as many Young Ones as three hands of fingers. Some of the Young Ones were babies, and some were Youngsters, and there were as many Olders as the fingers on one hand.

On this night the moon would be full, and The People would sit around the fire pit and Memory would tell one of their stories. This was an important event. For days the scouts and hunters had been out getting food, and the cookers had been making a feast. This was Oldest Boy's favorite time, and he didn't mind that he had been sent out to get firewood, even though that was usually a job for a Youngster.

Oldest Boy was even more excited than usual because the story tonight was his favorite, the Wolf Story. Oldest Boy had never seen a wolf. When he was a baby, The People had lived someplace else, and there were wolves there, but The People had left that place while he was still very little, and there were no wolves where they were now.

The feasting started in the late afternoon so that all The People would be finished eating when it was time for the moon to come up. It was a clear night in the time of year of The Moon When the Cold Begins to Go Away. Even though the snows were starting to melt, it was still cold. Usually, The People would stay inside their caves on a night like this, but none of the caves were big enough for all The People. That was why Oldest Boy and some others had spent all day gathering wood so the fire would be big enough to keep them all warm.

Oldest Boy enjoyed the feast and being together with all The People, but he kept looking toward the moon rise waiting for the first light to show. He wanted to hear about the wolves.

Finally, it was time, and Memory began her story in the traditional way.

"I am Memory, and this is a true story of The People. Listen carefully and learn, for what has happened before may happen again.

"For as long as I remember, and the Memory before me, and the Memory before him remember, The People lived near wolves. The Chiefs and the Scouts watched the wolves for many, many moon changes. They saw that the wolves were strong and fast and great hunters and that when they hunted, they went together and worked together to find and kill their prey.

"They saw that after the kill the wolves shared the food among each other and that they all brought food back for the young ones and the mothers and the wolves who were sick or hurt.

"They saw that the wolves loved their young and that they all helped to protect them and to teach them how to be a wolf.

"They saw all these things, and they came and talked to The People about it. The People decided that the wolves are just like us.

"In that time long ago, the Chief talked to Wise Mother to decide what to do. Wise Mother said, 'The wolves are our brothers and our sisters, and, if we help them, they will help us.'

"The Chief said, 'Wise Mother you are right. I must think about what we should do.'

"The Chief talked to the hunters and scouts about what to do, but no one had an idea. Then, one day, the Oldest Boy came to the Chief and said, 'Chief, I am sorry, but I have done wrong things, and I must tell you.'

"What have you done?" the Chief asked.

"Many times when I should have been working for The People I have instead gone and watched the wolves."

"I know this," the Chief said, "I have seen you. Why are you telling me now?"

"I think I know how the wolves and The People can hunt together and help each other."

"The Chief was a wise man, and he knew that, sometimes, even boys can have good ideas. He listened and liked what the Oldest Boy told him.

"That is why for more moons than any Memory could count The People followed the wolves when they went hunting. The People learned that the wolves could use their nose to find auroch or bison and chase them until they became tired and had to stop. But when the auroch or bison stopped running and huddled in a circle, they were hard for the wolves to kill.

"The People learned that if they followed the wolves, they would be able to kill as many animals as they wanted because the auroch or bison were all standing in one place and afraid of the wolves and not watching The People.

"The People would kill what they needed and cut up the meat to carry home, but they would always leave enough meat for all the wolves. Before long, the wolves would begin to howl when they were ready to hunt so The People could join them.

"The People never hunted the wolves, and the wolves never hurt any of The People. For many, many moons The People and the wolves were like brothers and sisters who lived apart in different homes, but hunted together and shared like family.

"Then one day, The People woke up, and the wolves were gone! No one knew where they had gone, but we soon discovered why they left. For days and days the scouts would go out and search for deer and auroch and bison, but there were only a few to be found. It became harder and harder to find enough food for The People. We don't know why, but many of the animals had left, and the wolves had followed them.

"Soon The People were hungry, and it was almost the time of the year of The Moon When the Leaves Go Red, and it would not be long before the cold.

"Our Chief said that we must leave our home and try to find the auroch and deer and bison and wolves so that we could eat. The People were sad. They didn't want to leave their home, but they knew that the Chief was right.

"That was many moon-changes ago when this Oldest Boy here was a baby. We found this place that has animals to hunt and good water and caves to live in. It is a good place, but there are no wolves here. We don't know why.

"Some of The People say that we did something to anger the wolves, but we don't know what. Every time the scouts and hunters go out, they look for a sign of wolves, but they have not found any.

"We will keep looking. Our lives are good, and the number of The People is many, but it is beginning to be harder and harder for the hunters and scouts to find animals for food, just as it was when the wolves left us. Chief and Wise Mother are worried that we may have to move again if we do not find the wolves to help us hunt.

"I am Memory, and this has been a true story of The People."

When Memory finished speaking The People were quiet. Many of them remembered the wolves and the good hunts they'd had with them. All of The People wished they could find the wolves again.

That night Oldest Boy lay under a bison hide blanket and thought about the Wolf Story. He wished he was a scout so he could go and look for the wolves. But if all of the scouts, grown men and women who knew so much more than he, could not find them, what chance would he have?

There was something that was keeping him awake, a feeling that he had. He didn't know this feeling. He'd never felt anything like this before, and he tried to understand why, but he couldn't. It wasn't until he was just drifting off into that hazy phase of sleep when the oldest, deepest part of the brain starts to take over that he knew.

The wolves were calling to him.

CHAPTER TWO

Runt

THE WOLF DEN WAS A BURROW dug into the side of a hill that rose just above the plain of tall grasses around it. There weren't many other hills around, and that's what made this hill important

From the top of their hill, the wolves could see far across the plains. More importantly, they could sniff the wind and get the scent of any animal for a long way around. This hill had been the center of the pack's territory for years.

In the den, the female nursed her litter of pups. This was her fourth litter, and it would be her last. She and her mate were getting old, and next year the pack would have new leaders. Soon after that, she would be gone. Knowing this did not worry her or make her sad. It was just the way of things.

The pups were eight weeks old now and starting to eat meat that other members of the pack brought back from the hunt, but they would continue to nurse for the next week or so.

Four of the pups, two males and two females, were busy suckling, but one pup was having trouble getting past them to get to a nipple. This pup was only a little more than half the size of the other four, and the mother wolf was worried about him.

Runts, wolf pups who were smaller than usual, often didn't survive. A wolf that couldn't do its share on the hunt was just another mouth to feed, and that wasn't something that a wolf pack living on the edge of starvation could afford.

Runts were sometimes killed by the lead wolf when times were bad. When her mate, the big, white wolf who was the pack leader, started sniffing around the little pup, she would growl and show her teeth. If he demanded it, she would have to let him kill the runt, but she hoped that wouldn't be necessary.

The winter that was hanging on into spring had been colder than usual. Cold winters were good for wolves. When it was cold, and the snow stayed on the ground for a long time, there was less forage for the plant-eaters, and they became weaker and easier to hunt. For some time now the pack had been able to find plenty of prey and the wolves were well-fed and content.

Hoping this would be enough to let her little pup survive, Mother pushed one of the larger pups aside with her nose to give Runt a chance to feed.

The weather grew warmer as spring gave way to summer and the puppies all grew. They were starting to venture out of the den and explore the area around Wolf Hill.

Runt was still much smaller than his brothers and sisters, but Mother was beginning to notice something unusual about him. He seemed to be practically fearless. Runt was always the first to explore something new and was the first to chase and kill a mouse. He also seemed to have more energy than the others. If he wasn't exploring, he was trying to get one of his brothers or one of the yearling wolves to play with him. He learned quickly. If he did something wrong and got a swat or a snarl from one of the wolves, he never did it again.

It had been some time since the leader, Big White, had looked at him with anything but affection.

Maybe he'll make it, Mother thought, *It depends on what happens when he starts to hunt with the pack.*

Four months later, Runt was growing every day, but he was still the smallest in his litter. That never bothered him. He was too busy exploring the world and learning new things.

In spite of their size, speed, and the strength of their jaws, wolves were cautious creatures. For a wolf, even a minor injury could be fatal. A broken tooth, a twisted knee, anything that could keep it from hunting could be a death sentence.

The Pack would care for an injured wolf as long as it could, but the needs of the Pack always came first. If food was in short supply and a wounded wolf was not healing, he or she would have to go. Most wolves would limp away on their own, never to be seen again. If a wolf did not leave voluntarily, he or she would be driven out.

That was The Law of the Pack, and, even at their early age, Runt and the other puppies knew it.

Because of this, wolves were suspicious of anything new and would usually avoid something they didn't know. Most of the pack preferred to stay with the other wolves on Wolf Hill when they weren't out hunting. Only the most experienced wolves, the Pack leaders, would leave the Pack to scout for new sources of food, and they would almost never travel alone.

Runt was different from the other wolves in the Pack. He was curious, adventurous and not afraid of being alone. When the other puppies were play-fighting or exploring near the den, Runt was wandering all over Wolf Hill smelling new smells and teaching himself how to hunt small creatures. He had already caught several mice and lots of lizards and large bugs. As a puppy, he was not required to share his kills. That meant that he always had extra meat and he was slowly gaining in size compared to his littermates.

When the puppies were out of the den, they were always being watched and guarded. Every wolf understood that the puppies were the future of the pack and that they had to be protected until they were big and strong enough to take care of themselves.

With Runt wandering all over the hill, he needed his own guard-wolf. The wolf who usually ended up with this job was Clown. He was the lowest ranking male in the pack. Clown never seemed to mind that he was always the last one to eat at a kill or that some of the other wolves snapped and snarled at him a lot. Clown just went his own way and tried to avoid wolves that might cause him trouble. He always did his share on the hunt, and he always gave some of his meat to the puppies, but he was happy to let the other wolves run the pack.

Clown liked Runt more than the other puppies. Clown was gentle with him, and he always saved him an extra piece of meat.

Even though he was different, all of the wolves of the Pack seemed to like Runt except one, Scar. Scar was two years old, and he was the largest male in the Pack except for Big White. Runt didn't worry that Scar didn't like him. Scar didn't seem to like any of the wolves.

When Scar was a yearling, he had stolen some meat from one of the older wolves at a kill. Scar got the meat, but that older wolf took a big piece of skin out of his side and the wound healed with an ugly scar. That was how he got his name.

Scar was a mean wolf.

Runt was patrolling along the bottom of Wolf Hill where the high grass came up to the bottom of the slope. Mice lived in the tall grass, and he was hoping to get an extra meal.

Suddenly, he caught a whiff of scent on the light breeze. Mouse! He froze with one paw still in the air and started working his nose. The mouse smell was coming from uphill and a little to his front. Perfect. He was downwind of the mouse, and that meant the mouse probably wouldn't be able to smell him. If he could work his way forward a few feet without spooking his prey, he'd be between the mouse and the tall grass. If he could keep the mouse out of the tall grass, Runt could catch it.

Runt slowly crept forward, moving only one paw at a time. If he could get just a couple more feet …

Runt's ears caught the faint sound of the mouse just above him. It sounded like it was chewing on something. Runt was in perfect position, he just had to be patient.

Wolf puppies aren't known for their patience. The others would have rushed up to get the mouse, and the mouse would have gotten away, but this was another way that Runt was different. He could think ahead and plan, and he knew that his best chance was to stay as still as possible.

After a minute the mouse finished what it was eating. Runt saw him stick his nose up from behind a small rock to test the breeze for any wolf scent, but Runt was still downwind, and the mouse didn't smell him. The mouse came trotting down the hill heading for the safety of the tall grass, and it never knew that Runt was there until it was too late.

With a quick leap and a snap, Runt caught the mouse and crushed it in his puppy jaws and went trotting up the hill with his head and tail high to show off his prize.

When he got to the top of the hill, he headed toward the den. He couldn't wait to show Mother his mouse. He was so pleased with himself that he didn't notice the look in Scar's eyes as he went trotting past. With no warning, Scar moved faster than a wolf should be able to and slammed into Runt and sent him flying through the air. He landed hard and rolled a few feet, and when he stopped and looked up Scar was standing over him and snarling.

Runt had no idea what was happening, but one look into Scar's eyes told him he was in trouble. Then Scar lowered his head and snapped at him barely short of his face. Runt was sure that the next snap of Scar's jaws would be around his head. He closed his eyes and peed on himself.

There was the sound of two bodies colliding above him, and when he opened his eyes Scar was on the ground a few feet away, and Clown was standing over Runt to protect him! Runt was glad that Clown had come to his rescue, but he was afraid of what would happen next. Clown was no match for Scar, and Runt could see by the look in Scar's eyes that he was ready to kill.

Before Scar could do anything, Runt heard the growl of another wolf and Mother came and stood over him next to Clown. Runt looked at Scar and could see that he was deciding whether he wanted to take on both Clown and Mother.

After a tense moment that seemed to drag on, Big White calmly walked up and positioned himself between Scar and the other two wolves. The crisis was over, but Runt and Clown had made a very dangerous enemy.

When he got up off the ground Runt was surprised to find that he still had the mouse in his mouth. He walked over to Clown and laid the mouse on the ground in front of him, and then reached up and licked Clown gently on the muzzle.

CHAPTER THREE

Clay

IT WAS A RAINY, WINDY DAY ON THE OUTER BANKS OF NORTH CAROLINA and Clay Webber was stuck inside the beach house with his sister and two girl cousins.

He didn't mind spending time with his sister and cousins. They were pretty good kids, but they were younger. Mara and Maia were both nine, and Iben was six. Besides, they were, well, girls. Clay was almost thirteen, and he'd been getting more and more interested in girls for the last year or so, but that meant girls in general, not these girls.

There were awnings on the porch that kept most of the rain out, but let in the breeze with the salty air from the ocean. The girls were playing a game on Mara's iPad and, judging by the laughter and giggles, enjoying themselves.

The adults were in the living room or kitchen.

Clay and the girls were at opposite ends of the screen porch. Usually, Clay would have either joined the girls or started reading a book. This morning he sat alone, lost in thought, remembering the strange events of the night before. It had started when Grandpa Sam's dog, Gunny, had come into his room and curled up on the floor at the foot of his bed.

Clay and Gunny had grown up together. Grandma liked to tell people about when they were very young. They were always together and almost always getting into trouble. Grandma says that she and Grandpa Sam called them "Captain Destructo and His Faithful K9 Companion Wreckit."

That was back when Clay's family lived near Grandma and Grandpa in Utah while Dad was going to law school there. They had moved around a lot since then. Clay's Dad was in the Marines and moving around was part of the job. Clay always thought about Gunny, and Gunny always remembered him whenever they got together. Gunny would jump up and lick Clay's face and then walk back and forth through his legs like Golden Retrievers do.

Gunny was getting old now, he was almost twelve. He had been a search and rescue dog almost his entire life, and that had been pretty hard on him. A year ago, a man kidnapped Grandma Rebecca and then shot Gunny when he came to help rescue her. Gunny had a big scar on his right hind leg, and he had to walk slowly, but he still liked to go out to the beach with Clay and the girls and wade in the surf.

What was strange about last night was that Gunny had never slept in the room with Clay before. Gunny almost always slept with Granpa and Grandma.

Even more strange was the dream Clay had. Except, dream wasn't the right word. He had been the Oldest Boy of The People, and he saw, everything through this other boy's eyes. It had seemed very realistic and, in some ways, it had been pretty cool to be living the life of a boy from long ago, but it had been disturbing, too. The People were worried because they couldn't find the wolves and they needed the wolves for hunting.

When Clay had first awoken and started thinking about this dream he thought it was silly. Humans don't hunt with wolves, they hunt with dogs. Then he realized that he hadn't seen a dog or any sign of dogs in the village. Why didn't they have dogs? Clay knew that humans had domesticated dogs a long time ago, but he wasn't sure exactly when or how.

Clay was a curious kid, and he wasn't going to let this go. He was going to figure out what this dream meant, but how?

Gunny had found Clay out on the porch and was keeping him company like he had when they were young. Clay looked down at Gunny and got the odd feeling that Gunny had something to do with his dream.

How could that be?

A couple of weeks ago, when they were getting ready for this trip to the beach, Clay thought about how good it would be to see Gunny again. Now that they were together, it was as if they had never been apart.

Clay leaned over to scratch Gunny's chest in the spot where he liked it the most.

I always knew that Gunny was something special, but that dream makes me realize how special all dogs are. I bet if The People had dogs they wouldn't have to go hunting with wolves. So why didn't they have dogs?

Where did you come from Gunny? How did we end up here together?

He was getting a little chilly, and starting to think about going in for a cup of hot chocolate when the door opened, and his Dad stuck his head out.

"Hey guys, our guest will be here in a few minutes. Finish up what you're doing and get ready to come in and pretend to be normal children."

My Dad, the comedian.

"Who's coming again?" Clay asked.

"For the tenth time, it's your Aunt Maddie's and Uncle Knut's friend from Oxford."

Dad was right, Clay hadn't been paying much attention when the adults had been talking about their guest, but then something he thought he remembered hearing made him ask, "What did you say this guy does?"

"He's a paleontologist, remember we talked about this."

"Yeah. They're the guys who study ancient animals, right?"

"Exactly. Now c'mon in. I think Grandma has some hot chocolate going."

Good old Grandma. Always knows when to make the hot chocolate.

The four kids sat at a table in the kitchen drinking their chocolate. The two Moms were being very strict about not allowing any drinks or messy food on the furniture. This was a rental house, they'd only be here for a week, and it wouldn't be good if someone spilled chocolate on a nice chair.

"What are we going to do now, Clay?" Iben asked.

"I guess that depends on what happens when your Mom's friend gets here," Clay answered.

Clay liked Iben, and he was always surprised at how well she spoke English. Clay's Aunt Maddie, his Dad's sister, had married a guy from Norway that she'd met when she was in school at Oxford University in England. Iben and her older sister, Maia, had been born in Oslo and lived there their whole lives. Maia and Iben only had a trace of an accent, but the way they talked sounded more formal. They always said "I have" instead of 'I've' and 'are not' instead of 'aren't' and things like that, but they could carry on a conversation in English better than most American kids.

On the other hand, when Maia and Iben were talking to each other in Norwegian, they might as well have been speaking Martian for all Clay could understand. They were pretty bright kids.

Clay's thoughts were interrupted when the doorbell rang.

The adults all got up, and there was a lot of chatter and hugging and handshaking. The man Clay saw didn't look like the other adults. He was tall with long hair, and he was wearing old scruffy cowboy boots, jeans, and a long-sleeved blue shirt. Not exactly beach attire. Finally, someone remembered the four kids.

Aunt Maddie brought the man over to introduce him.

"Guys this is our friend Doctor Cooper. He's going to be staying with us for a few days."

Doctor Cooper smiled a big grin and walked over to shake hands. When he got to Maia, she said, in her formal way, "I am very pleased to meet you, Doctor Cooper."

"Well, I'm very pleased to meet all of y'all too. But my friends call me Coop, so why don't we just stick to that?"

"You look like a cowboy," Mara said.

"I am a cowboy. I grew up on a ranch outside of San Antonio, and I learned to ride a horse almost before I learned to walk. I live over near El Paso now."

"Wow, that's cool!" Mara said.

"Are you here in case we get sick?" Iben asked.

"No, honey, I'm not that kind of doctor."

"He's a paleontologist."

"That's right, Clay. Do you know what that means?"

"It means you study ancient animals."

"That's right."

"OK, so where did dogs come from?"

"Whoa, pardner! I didn't know I was gonna have to take an oral exam before I even got unpacked. What brought that up?"

Clay hadn't expected this question and had to think fast, "Uh … I've been reading a lot about dogs and thinking about our dog Gunny, and I started trying to learn where dogs come from, but I haven't had much luck."

Hearing his name, Gunny walked over to investigate the stranger. Coop leaned down and gave him a good scratch behind the ears.

"I can tell you where this dog came from."

"Where?" Clay asked.

"He came from someone who knows how to breed good workin' dogs. He's a fine animal."

"He is not an animal!" Iben said, "He is a dog!"

"I'm sorry, Iben. He's a fine dog."

"Yeah, he's a search and rescue dog, and he's famous," Mara said.

"Really? That's interesting. I'd like to hear more about that."

"OK, guys. Let's give Coop a chance to get settled and talk with the grownups for a while."

"That's OK, Knut. I don't mind. I'm always happy to see kids who are curious about things. Are you ladies interested in learning more about where dogs came from?"

"Mom's taking us to the aquarium tomorrow," Mara said.

"What about you, Clay? Aquarium, or talk about dogs?"

"Talk about dogs!"

"OK, here's a deal for ya. You give me some time together with the adults for the rest of the day, and we'll schedule some time to talk tomorrow whenever you're not out at the beach, OK?"

Well, not really. I'd really like to talk right now, but I guess that's not gonna happen.

"Sure," Clay said.

"Good. You can tell me about your famous search dog, and I'll try to answer your question about where dogs came from," Coop said, sticking out his hand to shake, "Deal?"

Taking Coop's hand, Clay replied, "Deal."

The next day was sunny and beautiful, and Clay, Gunny, and the girls were out the door and heading to the beach as soon as they had gulped down some breakfast. Clay's Dad, Mike, and Grandpa Sam followed along to keep an eye on things.

There was a brisk on-shore breeze, and the waves were just right for riding a boogie board. Clay and his Dad paddled out into the surf while Grandpa worked with the girls a little closer to shore. Mara was pretty good with a boogie board, but Maia and Iben hadn't had many chances to try it. The water up in Norway was way too cold to go into with anything less than a full wetsuit. Mara spent most of her time with Maia while Grandpa worked with Iben.

From time to time Clay would look back at where Gunny was standing in the shallow water on the beach. Gunny wanted to come out and play with everyone else, but his injured leg wouldn't let him. That made Clay sad, so, after a while, he went in to take Gunny for a walk, and Mara went out to join her Dad.

They were all having so much fun that Clay almost forgot how excited he was to talk to Coop. After a couple of hours, it was time for a break and Clay ran back up to the house to find Coop, and the girls followed to get ready to go to the aquarium.

Coop and the others were sitting on the screen porch talking. Coop made Clay's day when he said, "Clay, you ready to talk about dogs?"

"Yes, sir! And I've got a bunch of questions!"

"Wait a minute there, buster," Hannah, Clay's Mom, said, "before you do anything, go to the outside shower and rinse off that sand and salt and make sure your Dad and everyone else does too. Then we'll see about talking with Doctor Cooper."

When Mom talked like that there was no sense in arguing, so Clay went to do as he was told.

It was almost an hour later before Clay finally sat down with Coop. His Grandpa Sam and Grandma Rebecca joined him, and Gunny tagged along. The Moms had gone to the aquarium with the girls, Dad and Knut were in the corner reading.

"OK," Clay said, "Tell me where dogs came from."

"Wait a minute, you go first. I want to hear about Gunny."

"That's what I brought Grandpa and Grandma for. They can tell you a lot better than I can."

"Great. Go ahead, Mr. Webber, Ma'am."

"Just Sam and Rebecca, please, Coop."

"Sure."

"Gunny and I have been doing search and rescue, SAR, for over eleven years now" Sam began, "We started off doing avalanche search at Snow Peak Ski Resort near where we live in Utah and then branched out to do wilderness live-find, wilderness cadaver, and water searches."

"He sounds like a pretty talented dog. How long did it take to train him?"

"About a year for avalanche search and then another year to get his other certifications."

"And where do you operate?"

"Well, besides Snow Peak we're with a K9 SAR team in northern Utah. Gunny and I have been on over eighty searches across Utah, Nevada, Wyoming, Idaho, and even up to Oregon."

"Wow. And this is all volunteer work?"

"Yep."

"That's impressive. What did he do to become famous?"

"Well, there were two what you might call high-profile searches. One was to the island of Iwo Jima. Are you familiar with that?"

"Sure, the battle of Iwo Jima where the Marines did that famous flag-raising on Mount Suribachi."

"Very good. I'm always surprised at how many people don't know enough history to know things like that."

"I enjoy reading history. I also know that you were a Marine like your son, Mike."

"Yeah, I was.

"Anyway," Sam continued, "We went to Iwo as part of a team that was looking for the remains of five Marines who'd been missing for over seventy years."

"And Gunny is able to find remains that old?"

"Older than that. Wait until I tell you my second story."

"OK"

"The team was me and Gunny, another former Marine with an explosive detection dog named Luke, a forensic anthropologist, a historian, and the team leader, a former Army Ranger. A Japanese forensic anthropologist joined us on Iwo."

"Pretty impressive group. Why the explosive dog?"

"Iwo Jima is a tiny island, eight square miles total. The U.S. alone dropped over twenty-thousand **tons** of explosives on that little rock. Not all of it went off. Our number one rule was that nobody went anywhere unless Luke had cleared it first. He found some artillery shells and one mine that might have killed Gunny."

"That's amazing. So, you found them?"

"Yeah, we had a good team, and we were successful. We found all five of the missing Marines and they were brought back to the U.S. for burial at Arlington National Cemetery."

"OK, now I remember seeing something about that on the news. Congratulations!"

"Yeah, well, Gunny and Luke get the credit. The rest of us were just in support."

"Gunny was able to find seventy-year-old remains just using his nose?"

"Yep"

With a little help from a ghost, Sam thought, *but I ain't talkin' about that.*

"What was the second search?"

"Have you ever heard of a place called the Medicine Wheel?"

"I don't think so."

"It's an ancient stone circle, kinda like a miniature version of Stonehenge, that sits high up in the Bighorn Mountains of Wyoming. The Indians call it the Buffalo Wheel. It's at least two thousand years old and it sacred to all of the Indian tribes of the Western U.S. It's now a National Historic Landmark."

"What happened there?"

"We were contacted by an Arapaho medicine man who said that there was a spiritual disturbance there that was causing a problem with some of their ceremonies. He thought that someone might have been buried there improperly. Turned out that someone might have been Butch Cassidy, the famous outlaw."

"Wait a minute, I thought Butch Cassidy and the Sundance Kid died in Bolivia back in the early 1900s."

"That's what we thought, too. We learned that there's a lot of evidence that Butch died in Wyoming or Utah in the mid-1930s."

"Wow."

"Yeah, so we had the same team as the one that went to Iwo Jima plus a third dog, a young dog named Iwo, who belonged to our forensic anthropologist."

"What happened?"

"Gunny and the other dogs found the grave, and we recovered the remains. But on our way out we got caught in a bad snowstorm, and then Rebecca got kidnapped by a meth dealer."

"Whoa, wait a minute. You're gonna have to explain all that. A snowstorm? What time of year was this?"

"Late June."

"A snowstorm in late June?"

"Yep, you can get snow any month of the year up in the Bighorns."

"OK, but what's this about a meth dealer?"

"It's a long story, but this was a really bad guy who got the idea that we were actually looking for buried treasure from one of Butch Cassidy's train robberies. He kidnapped Rebecca in the midst of this snowstorm and took off with her into the forest. Gunny was able to track him into the woods, and the three dogs were able to take him down before he could hurt Rebecca."

It was actually three dogs who turned into wolves, plus Sees Wolf's spirit wolf, hooxei, plus two ancient Arapaho warriors, but that's more stuff you don't need to know.

"Is that how Gunny was injured?"

"Yeah, that low-life tried to kill him."

"What happened to the meth dealer?"

"He didn't survive the experience."

"And was it Butch Cassidy?"

"Possibly. There was no evidence that it wasn't Butch, but the DNA tests were inconclusive."

"Boy, Gunny, you're quite a hero."

Gunny looked up at Coop and his face relaxed into a typical Golden Retriever grin.

Coop leaned over and scratched him behind the ears, "Good dog, good dog."

"OK," Clay said, "Now can we talk about where dogs came from?"

"Sure, Clay. Let me just take a quick break to get a cup of coffee."

Everyone else followed Coop out of the room to get a drink.

When everyone was back, Coop began, "Before we start, Clay, let me ask you some questions. What grade are you in?"

"I start eighth grade this year."

"What do you know about DNA?"

"A little, we studied it in science class last year. It's the stuff in our cells that's kinda like a blueprint for what we are. It tells the cells what to do when they divide."

"OK, sounds like you know the basics, so I'll let you decide if you want the eighth-grade version or the grown-up version."

"Do you have a grown-up version for someone who's not a paleontologist?"

"Yep, that's what we'll do.

"OK, I'll start with another question. How much difference in DNA do you think there is there between a Chihuahua and a Great Dane."

"I read that there's like less than one percent difference in the DNA of all dogs."

"Very good. That's right."

"Now we're getting' close to answering your question."

"Can you think of another animal whose DNA is less than one percent different from a dog's?"

"Uh ..., a wolf?"

"Yep, you got it. Wolves and dogs are so closely related that they can breed together. You know what breeding is, right?"

"Yeah, it means they can make babies, or puppies, I guess."

"That's it. What do you think that means for your question about where dogs come from?"

"Uh … that, …uh, dogs come from wolves?"

"Right! But, of course, it's a little more complicated than that, and there's a lot of stuff we don't know for sure. I'll try to give you the latest theories that actually sound pretty reasonable to me. OK?"

"Yeah, sure."

"We used to think that dogs are a domesticated version of the grey wolf or timber wolf. These are the wolves that are around today.

"But recent DNA studies have shown that both dogs and today's wolves came from an ancient wolf species that died out. Dogs and wolves came from the same ancestral wolf, and they are very closely related.

"With me so far?"

"Yeah, I think so, but here's another thing I don't understand. If dogs and grey wolves came from the same ancestor, how did dogs and wolves split off into two groups?"

"What you're really asking is how did wolves become domesticated and evolve into dogs?"

"Uh … yeah, I guess so."

"The answer to that question is that we're not really sure. Back when I was in college, we were taught that humans domesticated wolves, and there were a couple of theories about how we did that. Wanna hear?"

"Sure."

"One theory was that some humans decided that it would be a good thing to have some tame wolves around the cave. It's not clear why they would think this, but that was the idea. The theory was that these humans went out and stole some wolf puppies and brought them home and tamed them."

"OK, that makes sense."

"Yeah, the problem is that it's just about impossible to do. A lot of researchers have tried. Once a wolf puppy is old enough to survive without its mother's milk, it's one hundred percent wolf and impossible to domesticate. You might be able to tame it enough that it wouldn't try to eat you when it grew up, but then it would probably just run off.

"The other thought was that wolves started hanging around our caves and villages and eating some of the stuff we threw away. Eventually, the tamer wolves started coming closer and closer until they ended up living with us. This probably happened a lot throughout time, but we now think that most of those wolves ended up going back to the wild before they became anything like what we would think of as a dog."

"So, what did happen?"

"We're now beginning to think that we've been looking at it the wrong way around. The current theory is that we didn't domesticate the wolf, the wolf domesticated us."

"Huh?"

"Think about it. Back fifteen thousand or so years ago the human race was having a pretty tough time. We had not domesticated any animals, and we hadn't developed agriculture. We were still nomadic hunter-gatherers, and we were facing some pretty stiff competition from other animals that were a lot bigger and stronger than we were. On top of that, the world was going through a period of climate change that makes what's happening today look like nothing.

"Now, what if you had a wolf that was a little smarter, a little more adventurous than the other wolves, and he or she figured out that there might be some advantage to moving in with us. If the wolf made the first move, you wouldn't have to be very smart to figure out that having this critter around had some advantages for us too. All it would take would be for the right wolf to meet the right human."

"But how would something like that happen?"

"Maybe the best way to answer that is to tell you a story."

"OK."

"Imagine that you're a boy living in the Upper Pleistocene era, about fifteen thousand years ago, somewhere in what is now northern Europe. You're a human, a *Homo sapiens*, so you would look pretty much the way you do now except that you're dressed in animal furs, and you probably need a haircut. You've never had a bath or a shower except when it rains so your smell is, well … let's say natural. You're a part of an extended family group of about fifty people.

"There are three other boys and two girls about your age. You six are the next generation of the tribe's leaders, and you're spending almost all your time learning about hunting and food gathering.

"Your small group are the only humans for many miles around. In fact, you've only seen other humans from outside your group a few times in your life.

"With me so far?"

"Yeah, that sounds pretty cool. What do the girls look like?"

Coop grinned, "They're twins who look like Taylor Swift. They're on their smartphones all day, and they're really upset that no one is returning their texts. Why? What do you think they looked like?"

"OK, I guess they look like me except, … you know …?"

"They're girls?"

"Yeah."

"Yep, that's about right.

"So, one day you leave the village to go hunt for small game or maybe to look for some edible plants or something. As you walk along the trail you always take, a wolf comes out from behind a tree and stands in the open a short distance away. He's just a little farther away than you can throw your spear.

"In your first glance at this wolf, you immediately notice a few things. First, you've seen this wolf before. He and a couple of others have been hanging around your village for a while, but none of the wolves have come this close before. Next, you see that he's a he, not a female. He's only about the size of a German Shepherd, so he's still young, not fully grown. Then you realize that he's neither frightened of you nor being aggressive toward you. In fact, he seems curious."

"How would I know all those things in one glance?"

"Remember, you've lived in the wild around wild animals all your life. Your survival depends on being able to quickly identify which animals are threats, which are not threats, and which ones you might be able to hunt and kill.

"Tell me, how do you know when Gunny is hungry or when he needs to go out?"

"When he's hungry, he stands in the middle of the room, and he looks at you with a special look on his face. When he needs to go out, he stands by the door and looks back over his shoulder at you."

"Right, so you and Gunny have learned how to communicate with each other, right?"

"Yeah, so …"

"Animals communicate with their bodies and actions to each other all the time. If a deer ran away every time he saw a wolf or other dangerous animal, he'd spend all his time running and not enough time eating, and he'd die. A deer has to know how to tell if a wolf is hunting or if he has a full belly and he's just out for a stroll. As an early human, you would have learned at a young age all of the signs that animals give to each other."

"Wow, that'd be cool!"

"Yeah, and it's also likely that your sense of smell would have been a lot better than it is today. In fact, you probably would have smelled that wolf before you saw him if the wind was right."

"I'm not sure how cool that would be if no one had invented showers or soap yet."

"Point well taken. In any case, you might have been able to tell by his scent whether or not this wolf was a threat to you.

"Now you've seen this wolf and quickly decided that he's different from other wolves. He isn't a threat, and he seems curious. What do you do? And remember, this kid is just like you. He likes to learn new things."

"Maybe I squat down so he can see that I'm not gonna hurt him and I watch him for a while."

"Perfect! That's just what I hoped you'd do. What do you think happens next?"

"I dunno."

"Let's say you watch each other for a while, and the wolf relaxes and lies down, OK?"

"Yeah?"

"Then all of a sudden the wolf stands up, and you see his nose working, and he starts to move toward some tall grass nearby. You're worried for a second, but you see that the wolf isn't after you, he's spotted something in the grass. Then a big, fat rabbit jumps out of the grass right under the wolf's nose. The rabbit is so scared of the wolf that he's not thinking and he runs right toward you. The wolf starts to chase him, but he stops before he gets too close to you. You've got your spear handy —you've always got your spear handy — and that poor rabbit never knows what hit him.

"There you are with a dead rabbit on the end of your spear and a wolf about ten feet away who doesn't look quite as friendly as he did a few minutes ago. What do you do?"

"Uh … maybe I share the rabbit with the wolf?"

"Good idea. You take out your flint knife and slit the rabbit open and leave his guts on the ground. You walk backward a few steps and watch that wolf really, really closely. When you get far enough away, the wolf walks up and quickly gobbles down what you left him. Then he raises his head, and the two of you look into each other's eyes for the first time.

"And something clicks, a connection is made that no human has ever made with an animal before. The rest is history.

"You and that wolf don't know it, but you've just started the most successful partnership in the history of the world."

After the dramatic end of Coop's story, Clay was lost in thought for a minute, and then he said, "That's a great story, but it still doesn't explain how wolves became dogs, and how come that wolf didn't act like a normal wolf."

"You're right, that story was just the start. There's a lot more to it than that."

"OK, let's keep going."

Just then Grandpa spoke up.

"You guys may not have noticed, but it's lunchtime. Who wants to go with me down to the pier to get some fried oysters?"

"Aw, Grandpa, I wanna hear the rest of the story. Can you bring some back?"

Mike, Clay's Dad, replied, "No, come on, let's give Coop a break. I can eat some lunch too. You like oysters, Coop?"

"I've never had them fried, I'd like to try."

"How about you, Knut?"

"Sure."

"Mom?"

"No. You know I don't like oysters. You boys go ahead. I'll hold down the fort here."

"Let's go," Mike said, "We can finish talkin' when we come back — if Coop's willing, that is."

"Sure, I'm enjoying this. Don't worry Clay, we'll finish the story."

CHAPTER FOUR

Runt Leaves the Pack

WHILE THE HUMANS HAD BEEN TALKING, Gunny had been drifting in and out of sleep. He was always sort of half-listening to see if The Man would say that it was Time To Go To Work. Time To Go To Work meant that he and The Man would go out and search for a human that was missing. Searching with The Man was his favorite thing ever, and he kept hoping they would do it again, but they hadn't in a long time.

Gunny couldn't move very well since the Bad Man that was hurting Mom had shot him, but if The Man said it was Time To Go To Work, Gunny would go as fast as he could for as long as he could because he's a Good Dog.

After The Man and the other males left and he was alone with Mom, he let himself fall into a deeper sleep. All his life he had dreamed when he slept. His dreams used to be all about his favorite odors; the smell of the first human hand that had held him when he was born, or the smell of Old Bone that he searched for when The Man told him to Look Close and Adios. But for a while now, his dreams had been changing. Now his dreams had a lot of pictures in them, and they were becoming more and more real. Sometimes it didn't seem like a dream at all. It

49

was more like he was remembering something that he had done a long, long time ago. He saw things and smelled things he had never seen or smelled before, but he knew that they were real. He saw it all as it was happening, as he was doing it.

The strangest thing was that in his dreams he wasn't Gunny. He was a wolf named Runt.

He wasn't sure why he had gone into The Boy's room last night. The Boy was one of Gunny's favorite humans. They had played together when they were both puppies, and The Boy always treated him well. But Gunny didn't think that was why he was there. The Boy was beginning to remind him of someone else, another Boy that Gunny had known a long time ago, but couldn't quite remember. He thought that this other Boy had something to do with Runt, but he didn't know what. It was very confusing, so Gunny did what he usually did when he was confused or didn't understand something, he let himself drift off to sleep. Gunny was like most dogs. He believed that if something was meant to happen, it would happen and worrying about it wouldn't help. Better to sleep

Runt was now a yearling. For the last nine months, he had been growing and learning how to be a real wolf, a full member of the pack. He was still a little smaller than his littermates, but he wasn't a puppy anymore. He was about the size of a modern-day German Shepherd, and he was still growing.

As the winter was changing over to his second spring, he and his brother and sisters had gone on their first hunts with the pack.

He only had one brother now. His other brother had gone into the tall grass near Wolf Hill in the early part of winter and had never been seen again. Big White had led several adults out to look for him, but all they found were some spots of blood and the tracks of a big cat.

Big White and Mother had not had a litter this year. Instead, Scar had mated with another female and had a litter of six pups. It was clear that Scar would soon be the pack leader. Most of the wolves seemed unhappy about this, but that was The Law of the Pack — the strongest wolf must be the leader. All that was left was for Scar to show that he was stronger than Big White.

When the yearling wolves hunted with the pack, they were not expected to actually run down and kill the animal the pack was hunting. They were along mainly for training and were kept out on the flanks where they would be less likely to get in trouble and be hurt. Sometimes the deer or bison the pack was chasing would turn in an unexpected direction, and the yearlings would have to cut it off and run it back toward the rest of the pack, but they were never in for the kill.

When they hunted, Runt was the leader of the yearlings. Usually, the largest and strongest wolf of last year's litter would lead, but his littermates and the rest of the pack seemed to have given that role to Runt without any question. Runt had a natural sense of leadership and an understanding of how the pack hunted that typically only a seasoned adult wolf would have.

The two or three times when the prey had turned unexpectedly and seemed about to get away from the hunters, Runt had the yearlings in just the right position to turn the animal back into the pack.

Once the prey was down, the pack started to feed. The leaders, Big White, Mother, Scar and a couple of others ate their fill first. The yearlings ate with the lower ranking wolves. As the lowest ranking wolf, Clown should have waited until all the other wolves had fed, but Runt always let Clown eat alongside him. This wasn't a violation of The Law of the Pack, but it was something new and different, and, at first, the wolves were uncertain and suspicious. But, as Runt's reputation as the leader of the yearlings grew, this strange practice was accepted by all of the wolves in the pack.

All of the wolves except Scar.

Runt was surprised that Scar hadn't confronted him. After a while, he realized that Scar was biding his time. Scar had another confrontation coming with Big White that he would have to settle first. Runt knew that Scar would find time for him later.

Summer arrived after a winter that had been milder than last, and the wolves had to work harder to find the food they needed. They had been able to get enough to eat but just barely. No wolf was going hungry, but none was getting fat, either. There was a constant sense of worry in the pack about food and the battle between Scar and Big White that they all knew was coming.

It was a hot afternoon when it finally happened. This time of year, the pack hunted mainly in the evening and early morning and rested during the heat of the day. It had been a couple of days since the last successful hunt. Not long enough to cause a problem, but long enough to make the pack more worried than usual.

While the rest of the wolves dozed in the warm sun, Runt was moving around the hill hunting for mice just as he had when he was a puppy. Runt didn't know if the small extra meal he got from a mouse was worth the energy he expended in catching it, but he was restless and had to be doing something. This was one more thing that made him different from the other wolves.

Runt had gone around and checked all the usual places where there were mice and found no sign of anything. After two turns around the hill, he gave up and headed back toward the rest of the pack near the top. As he approached a group of sleeping wolves, a fat little mouse ran out from behind some rocks right in front of him. The mouse was running toward the sleeping wolves, and Runt ran to catch him before one of the others could. He was about to grab the mouse when he saw from the corner of his eye Scar running toward him. He thought that Scar was going after the mouse too, so he ran faster, but he was wrong. Scar didn't want the mouse.

Scar wanted him.

Runt's nose was just an inch from the mouse when Scar crashed into his side. Runt was bigger and stronger than he had been the last time Scar attacked him, and he was able to keep his balance, and instead of being knocked down he was able to turn to meet Scar's attack. Runt couldn't hope to beat Scar in a fight. His only chance was to make Scar think that he could hurt him and make him back off.

It almost worked.

The two wolves stood a few feet apart snarling at each other. Runt knew that Scar had two options. If he attacked and beat Runt, which he could easily do, he would demonstrate his strength to the pack, but if he was hurt seriously enough, it could mean his death. If he turned away from Runt, he would look weak and lose the respect of the other wolves.

Runt could see that Scar was trying to decide what he should do. Just then, Mother charged up to protect her favorite from her last litter. Scar saw his chance, and he quickly turned from Runt and charged at Mother raking her with his teeth along her left shoulder and leaving a deep gash. Just as quickly he jumped away before Runt or Mother could fight back.

The stage was set for the showdown to determine who would lead the pack. Big White couldn't allow his mate to be attacked and not defend her. He would have to fight Scar whether he was ready or not.

For Scar, the chance to fight Big White was worth the risk of injury. The winner would be the pack leader.

Big White trotted calmly up to where the three wolves stood facing each other. Runt wanted to join him to challenge Scar together, but with a look and a snarl, Big White told him to stay away. This had to be between Big White and Scar. That was The Law of the Pack.

As the two wolves moved toward each other the rest of the pack gathered around. Most of them had known only Big White as pack leader. If that were going to change it would have a major impact on their lives.

Scar was a mean and selfish wolf, but he was smart. Big White was as strong as he was and more experienced, but Scar was young and quicker, and that was his advantage. Instead of attacking directly, he began to circle the other wolf looking for an opening. It didn't take long.

When Mother tried to move to where she could watch better, she put too much weight on her injured leg and made a small whimper. Big White's eyes flicked toward his mate.

In that instant when Big White's attention was diverted, Scar attacked. Instead of going for a killing bite to the neck he went to Big

White's exposed hip. He slashed quickly with his teeth and then jumped away before Big White could turn to attack.

Big White was hurt. Not seriously, but enough that he was slowed, giving even more speed advantage to Scar.

After that, there was no doubt about the outcome. Scar made two more attacks giving Big White two more minor wounds, and then stood still daring the older wolf to attack him.

If Big White continued to fight, he could be seriously injured or killed. That would mean that Mother would be on her own because Scar would undoubtedly drive her out of the pack. He had no choice. Turning his back on Scar, Big White walked to Mother, and the two of them limped out of the circle of wolves and out of the pack.

When Scar saw that Big White and Mother were leaving, he sat on his haunches, lifted his muzzle to the sky and began to howl in victory. A few of the wolves joined in half-heartedly. Runt ignored all of them and began to trot after Big White and Mother. He would not let them face the dangers outside the pack when they were alone and injured. Before he had gone far, another wolf joined him. Runt didn't have to look to know that Clown was alongside him.

When they had almost caught up with the other wolves, Big White spun around suddenly and faced them snarling. Runt was confused. Didn't Big White want their help? He stared at Big White's angry snarling face for a moment, and then he understood.

It was The Law of the Pack. Big White had been beaten by Scar who was now the pack leader. He and Mother were injured and couldn't hunt, and food was in short supply. Even though he was no longer the pack leader, Big White's first priority was always the welfare of the pack. He and Mother would leave for the good of all, and he would not allow two healthy wolves who could hunt and help the pack to leave with them.

When Big White saw that Runt understood, he relaxed, and the snarl left his face. Runt and Big White looked sadly at each other for a long minute. Mother limped forward until her nose was touching Runt's. She licked him on the muzzle for the last time. She walked to Clown and licked his muzzle as well. Then the two old wolves turned and limped into the tall grass.

When Runt and Clown walked back up to the top of the hill, Scar was waiting for them. The look he gave them was one of pure hatred. Runt didn't think that Scar would do anything now when the pack needed all of its wolves healthy for the hunt, but he and Clown would eventually pay the price for their loyalty to Big White and Mother.

The next morning when the pack was setting out to hunt, Runt took his place as the leader of the yearlings. When he did, Scar ran over snapping and snarling and pushed him away. Scar made it clear that Runt was no longer a leader, and he put Runt's brother in his place.

Runt didn't like the way that Scar led the pack on the hunt. He relied too much on speed and strength and too little on planning. Several times Scar pushed the wolves to near exhaustion chasing a healthy animal that they couldn't catch. Runt saw that Scar sometimes passed up a chance to go after an older or slower animal. Runt didn't understand this. He was beginning to think that there was something wrong with Scar. Something that might cause trouble for the pack.

But what could he do?

By the time summer was coming to an end, the pack was in bad shape. More and more of their hunts had been unsuccessful, and the wolves were beginning to look thin and scraggly. The only ones that were well fed were the puppies and their mother, and Scar and two other wolves. These two wolves had supported Scar in every dispute within the pack. As the highest ranking wolves in the new pack order, these three always fed first at every kill and were able to fill their bellies.

Runt and Clown were now the two lowest ranking wolves in the pack, which meant that they got the least food. Runt was still able to catch mice and lizards, but he had to be careful. He wasn't a puppy any longer, and he was expected to share anything he killed with the rest of the pack, although how he could share a mouse with a bunch of hungry wolves was beyond him. He did share with Clown and the few extra bites of food they got helped keep them from starving.

On a cold day in early winter just after the first snows, Runt was out hunting for mice again. Clown had joined him because he was hungry. Yesterday's hunt had been a failure, and the wolves were getting desperate.

Runt and Clown had found all the mice around Wolf Hill, and they had started going out into the tall grass. Young wolves were not supposed to go this far on their own, but they knew that the rest of the pack was too tired and hungry to care.

Runt had been going along with his nose close to the ground sniffing for mice. He would raise his nose every few seconds to test the wind for other scent. He hadn't forgotten what had happened to his brother in the tall grass.

When he raised his nose the next time, he caught a new scent on the slight breeze. Deer! There was a deer somewhere close, and he was upwind of Runt and Clown. Runt didn't know why there would be a deer this close to Wolf Hill, but that didn't matter. The deer was here, and, if he and Clown could catch him, there might be enough meat for the whole pack.

Runt saw Clown's nose twitching and that he had caught the scent of the deer. With a nod of his head, Runt told Clown to stay where he was. Runt then started circling to get around on the other side of the deer. If he could get the deer between the two of them, they'd have a chance to catch it.

Runt moved as quietly and smoothly as he could. When he got out to the side of the deer, he lost the scent, but his sharp ears could hear the deer's movements. It sounded like the deer was eating and it wasn't very quiet or observant. There must be something wrong with a deer that was this careless so close to Wolf Hill.

In a few minutes, he was almost upwind of the deer, and it would get his scent any second. And there! The deer's head popped up and swiveled back to look at Runt. As the deer sprang away, Runt saw its problem. It was a young deer, a yearling like Runt. It must have gotten separated from its herd, and it was too young to have learned what it needed to know about wolves.

The deer ran from Runt and right at Clown. Clown may have had a low rank in the pack, but he was still a big, strong wolf. The deer never knew that Clown was there until his jaws latched onto its neck, and then it was over.

Runt and Clown stood looking at the dead deer. It was fat and healthy with plenty of meat on it. It was Runt's first real kill, but he felt no excitement. He was much too hungry for that. He should go immediately and tell the pack so they could all come and feed, but there was no way he could leave this feast without taking at least enough to dull his hunger.

He and Clown quickly tore off a few choice bits of meat and gobbled them down. Then Runt lay on top of the deer and rolled around to get the animal's scent on him, and trotted off to the pack.

Runt had just started up Wolf Hill when the pack caught the fresh scent of deer on him and came running down to investigate. The wolves all crowded around him to get the smell. They knew what it meant. There was food out there, and Runt would lead them to it.

Runt turned and led the pack out for their first real meal in a long time.

Scar and his friends had insisted on eating first, and the other wolves let them because that was The Law of the Pack, but Runt could see that most of the wolves resented it.

Finding this food for the pack when Scar had been unsuccessful on so many hunts made Scar hate Runt even more. Scar was beginning to see him as a rival for pack leader.

Although Runt had no interest in being the pack leader, it was clear that many of the other wolves were beginning to hope that he would — not right away, he was too young — but soon. Runt was becoming afraid that the pack was splitting, and, with winter coming soon, that wouldn't be good. The pack would need all of its wolves to be healthy and work together to get through the difficult days ahead. Like Big White, Runt's first concern was for the welfare of the pack.

Scar's first concern was Scar, and he would do anything to keep his position at the head of the pack. Runt knew that another confrontation with Scar was coming soon.

Over the next month, the pack was more fortunate in its hunts. The other yearlings made Runt their leader again, and Scar didn't stop them. Now that Runt understood how Scar hunted, he was able to get the yearlings into position to better help the pack. Twice the yearlings actually made the kill. One of these kills was a young bison who provided more meat than the wolves had gotten since Big White had left.

While the rest of the pack was happy, Scar was becoming angrier. It was unheard of for a yearling to be the pack leader, not to mention a yearling who was also a runt, but that seemed to be what the pack was thinking. Even Scar's closest supporters seemed to be acting friendly toward Runt. Scar wanted to confront him, but he was afraid that the rest of the pack wouldn't back him. Runt was sure that Scar was trying to find some way to get rid of him without having a one-on-one fight.

It was Clown who gave Scar the chance he was looking for.

It was a cold day with a light cover of snow on the ground, but the sun made it feel warmer than it was. Clown was lying near one of the burrows that the wolves used to get out of the cold and chewing on a bone that still had a bit of meat on it. The pack had completed another successful hunt, and the wolves were all relaxing with full bellies.

Scar trotted up to Clown and growled down at him. He was demanding that Clown give him the bone. This was something that the pack leader had the right to do, but not something that Big White had ever done.

Maybe Clown really wanted that bone, or maybe he was finally sick of being pushed around by Scar. Whatever the reason, Clown didn't give up the bone, and he snarled back at Scar in defiance.

Scar didn't hesitate. Without warning he attacked, and his first strike opened a big gash on Clown's shoulder and knocked him to the ground. Scar was tensed to attack again when Runt barrelled into him and knocked him off his feet.

Runt took a position between Scar and Clown defending his friend. They both held their ground while the rest of the pack gathered around.

Now Runt was in the same position that Big White had been. He probably couldn't beat Scar in a fight, and there was a good chance that Scar would hurt him badly. Then Scar would banish Runt and Clown from the pack, and they would be on their own. Two injured wolves would have little chance of surviving the winter on their own.

A couple of weeks earlier the pack might have supported Runt against Scar, but now that their bellies were full they were less likely to take a chance on a new pack leader. Runt was on his own.

Runt slowly backed away keeping his eyes on Scar. When he got next to Clown, they both backed away together until they could see Scar relax. Then they turned and walked down Wolf Hill for the last time.

Runt and Clown walked toward the place where the sun comes up until Wolf Hill was out of sight. Runt had not chosen to go that direction for any particular reason, he just needed to move, and he wanted to get as far away from the pack as he could.

Runt was so caught up in his own thoughts that he didn't pay attention to Clown until he heard him make a soft whine. Runt looked at his friend and saw that his shoulder was bleeding, and he was limping. Runt quickly found a small pile of soft snow and motioned for Clown to lie down. Clown put his injured shoulder down and gave a sigh of relief as he sank slowly into the bed of snow.

They couldn't stay there long. The other wolves would give them some time to get out of the pack's territory, but not long. A banished wolf was considered an enemy of the pack, and they could be killed if Scar brought the pack out after them, but Runt had to give Clown some time to rest his injured shoulder.

Runt had never wanted to be a pack leader, but now he was. His pack was just him and an injured wolf, but that didn't matter. Runt had to do whatever was needed to see that his pack survived.

While Clown rested, Runt began to plan. From Wolf Hill, the pack hunted the mostly-flat, grassy plain that stretched for as far as they could see from the top of the hill. Runt didn't know how far the pack's territory extended. There was only one place where the pack always stopped and went no farther. In the direction of the place where the sun comes up there was a river and on the other side of that river were trees, many trees crowded together in a forest, thick and dark. The pack would often go to the river to drink and, sometimes, swim, but none of the wolves had ever gone to the other side.

The pack had lived on Wolf Hill and hunted in the grassy plains for so long that none of the wolves now alive had ever been in a forest, and the idea of going there was frightening to them, but Runt wasn't afraid. The two or three times he'd been to the river he'd wanted to go across and explore in the trees, but he'd have been punished if he tried.

Now he realized that the only place he and Clown would be safe was in the forest. He didn't know what they would find there, but he knew what would happen if they stayed in the plains.

As soon as Clown could move, they would continue toward the trees.

When the cold snow had eased the pain in his shoulder, Clown stood. Runt looked at his friend and saw that he was walking with a limp and must be in pain, but it seemed like the bleeding had stopped. Runt tried to set a slow but steady pace that Clown could match without hurting himself more.

The two walked along until the sun was almost down. Runt found a small hill and climbed to the top to check for scent in the wind. The wind was coming from back toward Wolf Hill, and Runt could smell many different animals but no wolf scent. The pack wasn't after them.

Even though it was early in the winter, it would get cold when the sun was down. Clown was looking tired, and, since there was no sign they were being followed, Runt decided to rest for the night.

On the lee side of the hill, Runt found a drift of snow piled up by the wind and began to dig. Soon he had a burrow large enough for the two of them to get in. He motioned Clown in and then crawled in after him. They were sheltered from the wind, and their thick fur coats would keep them warm in their snow cave. The two wolves curled up together, and Clown almost immediately went to sleep. Runt lay awake, thinking and planning.

The first thing they had to do was get across the river. Runt wasn't sure how far away it was, but it took the pack a full day to get there running at a lope. Wolves could lope for hours at a time and cover vast distances. Runt and Clown had been walking much more slowly for less than half a day, but they had been moving in more or less a straight line. When the pack was hunting, they ran in one direction then another following scent and searching for prey. Runt thought that he and Clown could make it to the river by the time the sun went down tomorrow.

Their bellies were still pretty full, so food was not an immediate problem, and there were plenty of small ponds and puddles so they would have water. Runt was pretty sure that they would be able to spend tomorrow night in the forest.

With his mind at ease, Runt drifted off to sleep alongside his friend.

The next morning Runt woke before the sun was up and eased his way out of the burrow trying not to disturb Clown. Clown had a long, hard day ahead and Runt wanted him to rest as much as he could.

In the dim, pre-dawn light outside the burrow, everything looked grey and white. Runt sniffed the air and didn't smell anything that might be either a threat or food, but he did smell snow. There was a storm coming.

Clown crawled out of the burrow as the sun was coming up. He was moving stiffly and slowly, but there was only a little blood in the snow where he'd slept, and he didn't look sick. It would be a hard day for Clown, but he'd make it if they didn't run into problems.

When Clown was ready, Runt started off at a slow walk. As Clown's shoulder became less stiff, they moved a little faster. Runt looked for the most natural path to follow. From time to time they found animal trails they could use and once they followed the trail left by a herd of mammoth that was smooth and made walking easy. Runt kept an eye on Clown, and when he saw that he was struggling, they would stop and rest. Runt always found a pile of snow that Clown could lie in to ease his pain.

The wind that had been steady from the west was now changing and blowing in all directions. This was good because it let Runt know if there was anything dangerous or edible anywhere around them. So far Runt hadn't smelled anything of interest. There had been some snow, but it didn't look like they would have a big storm soon.

It was late in the afternoon when Runt saw something new on the horizon. Soon he could clearly see the tops of trees being blown in the wind. Clown whined, and Runt turned to see if he was having trouble, but his friend was just looking anxiously at the trees. It was clear that Clown wasn't nearly as confident about going into the forest as Runt.

It wasn't long before they came to the river. It was about as broad as five or six of Runt's running strides, and it looked deep, but Runt wasn't worried about that. Wolves are good swimmers.

His problem was going to be convincing Clown to go across to the side where the forest was.

The two wolves stood on the riverbank for a long time. Runt wanted to get moving so that they would have time to dry off before it got dark and colder, but he couldn't rush Clown. Clown was an easygoing, amiable wolf, but he wasn't stupid. They had to cross the river and leave the pack's territory. Runt would give him some time to make up his mind.

Finally, Clown stepped up to the water's edge, closed his eyes and jumped as far out into the river as he could and started paddling furiously. Runt quickly followed.

It only took a couple of minutes for the two wolves to swim across, and as they stood shaking their fur and panting Runt realized that he had just started a new life. He and Clown were on their own and whether they would live or die would be entirely up to them. It was scary, but it was exciting too.

For the first time in his life, Runt sat back on his haunches, raised his muzzle to the sky, and howled like an adult wolf.

With darkness coming, neither wolf wanted to begin exploring the forest, but they had to find some shelter. There was a narrow strip of land maybe twice as wide as the river where there were only a few scattered trees before the true forest began. Close to where the forest started, several trees had fallen, and one of them looked like someplace where they could find shelter.

When Runt checked the tree, he saw a mound of snow under a cover of branches that looked promising. When he got closer, he caught a scent. Rabbit! Runt froze and put his nose to work. He soon figured out that there was a rabbit in a small burrow just under the snow. If he could get closer before the rabbit realized he was there….

Runt trotted happily back to Clown with the rabbit in his jaws. One rabbit wasn't a big meal for two wolves, but it was a lot better than nothing. They had worked hard on their walk, and they needed something to eat. Runt and Clown ate like hungry wolves.

It was completely dark by the time the rabbit was finished, and Runt led Clown back to the snow pile under the fallen tree. In a few minutes, Runt had a burrow dug out for them, and they both crawled inside and curled up together. As he had the night before, Clown went to sleep almost immediately.

As he listened to Clown's slow breathing, Runt thought back on the last two days. He was almost happy at the way things had turned out. He missed the pack, especially his brother and sisters, but he had known that this day was coming for some time. When it came to a showdown, Clown was the only wolf who stood beside him. The other wolves didn't think much of Clown. He was too … nice. But Runt doubted that many of those wolves could have made the walk they had made that day with Clown's badly injured shoulder.

They had done what they had to do. They were out of the pack's territory, they had a whole new world in front of them, and they had managed to find a meal.

Runt was beginning to think that they just might make it.

The pain in his injured hip woke Gunny up. He usually had to get up every hour or so to change positions because something hurt. If he had been just an average dog, he wouldn't have so many injuries, but then he wouldn't have the memories of all the times he and The Man had gone up into the mountains to find someone who was lost. The memories were worth the pain.

He shifted into a position that was comfortable and lay there thinking about his dream. Usually, a dream was about something that he was doing, but when he dreamed about Runt and Clown and Big White and the others, he saw everything as it happened through Runt's eyes, he smelled everything with Runt's nose and heard everything with Runt's ears. He also knew Runt's thoughts and feelings. When Runt was happy, it made Gunny feel good. When Runt was sad, especially when Big White and Mother left the pack, it made Gunny feel bad.

Gunny didn't know if he liked having these dreams or not, but one thing was sure. He hoped he had more of them because he had to find out what happened to Runt and Clown.

He was about to fall back asleep when he heard The Man and The Boy and the other males coming back, and he slowly got himself up and went to see if they had brought him any food.

CHAPTER FIVE

Genetic Mutation

CLAY ENJOYED HAVING LUNCH WITH HIS DAD, Grandpa Sam, Knut, and Coop. There had been a lot of talking, and Clay had felt like he'd been included in the conversation with the men. They sat outside at a table on the pier, and all of them had eaten fried oysters with french fries and cole slaw. He used to think that eating something like an oyster was yucky, but that was before his Dad had given him his first North Carolina fried oyster. Now he ate them whenever he could. He still wasn't too sure about trying a raw oyster, though, and when Uncle Knut told him about Norwegian lutefisk, he was sure he was never going to eat that.

Clay had promised Dad not to bother Coop with a lot of questions about dogs, and he had been pretty good about that, but he hoped they would be able to start again as soon as they got back to the beach house. It didn't work out that way.

Mom, Aunt Maddie, and the girls got back to the house from the aquarium shortly after Clay and the men. They all had gotten souvenirs at the gift shop. Iben had gotten Clay a book about sharks, and he thought it was pretty nice of Iben, even if he figured his Mom had paid for it.

The girls all wanted to play with their new toys, and Clay wanted to talk with Coop, but the Moms said in no uncertain terms that they weren't paying thousands of dollars for this beach house and not spending any time on the beach. They were all going to go to the beach, and they were all going to have fun, and that was that.

Once again, there was no sense arguing. He saw Coop give him a wink that he took to mean, "Don't worry, we'll have plenty of time to talk," and that made him feel a little better.

Besides, there were worse things than having to go out and play on the almost-empty beaches of the Outer Banks.

The wind had died down, and there weren't any waves for boogie boarding so they mostly just swam. Clay helped the girls build a couple of sand castles, and he spent some time playing catch with his Dad. Gunny was even able to get in the calm water for a swim.

After a couple of hours, everyone was ready to get in out of the sun for a while. By the time they had finished showering and cleaning up there was an hour or so left before dinner time, and Clay went looking for Coop. He found him in a shady spot on the porch with the other men.

"Looking for me, Clay?"

"Yes, sir. Do you have some time to talk to me about why that wolf in your story was different from other wolves?"

"Sure. Is it OK with the rest of you if Clay and I talk? I don't want to bother you."

"No, go ahead," Mike said, "I'm actually interested in hearing about this myself."

When Coop saw Sam and Knut nod their heads in agreement, he closed his eyes for a moment to gather his thoughts.

"OK, you asked how the wolf could become a dog, and why the wolf in my story wasn't afraid of men like the other wolves were?"

"Yes, sir."

"The answer is genetic mutation."

"You mean like when somebody is exposed to radiation or some virus, and they get turned into a zombie or somethin'?"

Coop chuckled, "No. Genes can be changed by things like radiation, but that's not what I'm talkin' about, and, as far as I know, there's no such thing as a zombie."

"Darn!"

"When I talk about genetic mutation, I mean that something is changed in an animal's DNA when it's passed down from a parent to an offspring."

"Why does that happen?"

"We get our genes from our parents. You inherited your Dad's gene for dark hair, and Mara inherited your Mom's gene for lighter hair. Sometimes genes can skip a generation or two, and you might inherit a gene from one of your grandparents. You end up being a combination of several of your ancestors, and that's why we have so many different kinds of people in the world, and we don't all look and act the same."

"Yeah, OK, I understand that."

"But sometimes we inherit a gene that's different from any of our ancestors' genes. A gene that's been changed or mutated."

"Why does that happen?"

71

"Well, it can happen the way you described it. One of your parent's genes could have been damaged by something, and you inherit that, or sometimes it's just random."

"What do you mean? How can things just happen at random?"

"DNA is complicated with billions of pieces. With something like that there's a chance for errors, mistakes."

"Isn't that bad?"

"It can be. You could inherit some genetic disease like Down Syndrome, but most of the time these genetic mutations don't have any effect at all, and sometimes the effect can be beneficial."

"Like what?"

"Like making you a little less fearful than the other wolves in your pack."

"But genes don't determine whether a wolf is afraid of a man or not do they?"

"Sure they do. At least in part. This is a new area, and we still don't know a lot about the role that genes play in our emotions, but we do know that they play a role, and we're learning more about that every day. For example, we know that mice whose brain cells lack a receptor for a certain chemical are more fearful than other mice, and they're missing this receptor because of a difference in one of their genes."

"You're saying that the wolf in your story wasn't afraid of the boy because he had a gene that was different from other wolves."

"Yep. That's the basic idea. And if that wolf met another wolf with the same gene and they mated and had puppies, and some or all of those puppies got that gene, well the next thing you know you've got a bunch of wolves that aren't afraid to hang around near humans. And if those wolves and the humans saw that there was some advantage to their two species being together, maybe hunting together, maybe helping to protect each other, then you've got the makings for evolutionary change."

"OK, but there's a lot of ifs and maybes in what you just said."

Coop looked over at Mike and asked, "Is he always this big a pain in the butt?"

"Yeah, pretty much," Mike replied, "You get used to it after a while."

"OK, Clay you're right. There's a lot of ifs and maybes. But we're not talkin' about one wolf and one human, we're talkin' about hundreds, maybe thousands, of encounters. All it would have taken would be for a few of these encounters to be successful, and fifteen thousand years later you've got a world full of dogs."

"OK, but we have a world full of dogs, not a world full of tame wolves. How did wolves become dogs?"

Just then Clay's Mom yelled from the kitchen, "Dinner in five minutes. Go get cleaned up."

Coop smiled at Clay, "Saved by the bell. We'll finish this tomorrow."

Clay frowned and pretended to be upset, but he had a lot to think about before his next session with Coop.

Clay's small bedroom was on the top floor of the house. The air conditioning didn't reach up that far very well, but he had a window on the beach-side that he could open. He liked the fresh ocean air better than the air conditioning anyway.

Once again, Gunny had come up with him and curled up on the floor at the foot of his bed. Clay didn't know why, but he had a feeling that Gunny was here because of something to do with all the stuff he and Coop had been talking about.

Clay lay awake for almost an hour going back over what Coop had told him. He wished that his teachers at school were all like Coop because he'd learned a lot in the last two days.

As he got drowsy, he wondered whether he would have any more strange dreams about Oldest Boy. The dream, or whatever it was, the night before had been interesting, and he thought he'd like to find out more about what happened with The People and the wolves.

At the foot of Clay's bed, Gunny was already asleep and dreaming. His dream was about Runt and Clown, but it wasn't really a dream. It was something else.

CHAPTER SIX

Sweetbreath

RUNT DIDN'T WAKE UP BEFORE DAWN THE NEXT MORNING as he usually did. When he did wake, he saw why. The entry to their burrow was covered with snow, and it was still dark inside. When he dug his way out, he saw that it was snowing.

Clown was still sleeping. Runt sniffed around Clown's nose and on his injured shoulder. About two moon-changes ago, one of the pack's wolves had been cut by the antler of a large deer during a hunt. He didn't seem to be hurt too badly, but after a few days the wound began to make a bad smell, and two days later the wolf was dead.

Runt didn't detect any of that bad smell on Clown, and he decided that the best thing to do was just to let him rest.

Runt eased his way out of their den. As soon as his nose was outside, he started sniffing. There were several different animal scents, but none were too near or smelled dangerous. He came all of the way out and stood in the snow looking and listening. When he was confident that there was nothing nearby to worry about, he trotted over to the edge of the forest and lifted his leg on three or four trees. He did this partly to start marking his new territory and partly because he just had to pee.

Runt walked a short distance into the trees and immediately felt the difference between the forest and the plains where he had lived his whole life. There were new odors from plants and animals he had never encountered before, and the thick trees blocked his view in every direction. In the plains, the tall grass often blocked his line of sight, but he could usually find a small hill that would get him high enough to be able to see. In the forest there were a few low mounds, but nothing that would be high enough to give a wolf much of a vantage point.

Most wolves would be frightened by something so new and strange. The other wolves in the pack would be very nervous to be standing where he was.

Runt wasn't nervous. He was alert and cautious, but most of all he was interested and excited. He wanted to get into this forest and explore, but that wouldn't be the smart thing to do right now.

An unknown forest was not the place for a young wolf to be on his own. Runt's first priority was to help Clown get healthy so the two of them could work together. That meant Runt had to do two things right away. First, he had to find a spot for a better, safer den, and then he had to find a regular source of food. And he had to do this on his own without getting too far away from Clown. With his injury, Clown was no longer a predator; he was prey. Runt had to protect him.

The only thing about his new situation that really scared Runt was losing Clown and being on his own. He couldn't let that happen.

With all this on his mind, Runt began to carefully check out his new territory. He worked mostly along the edge of the trees and not too far into the forest, searching and sniffing for a while and then circling back to check on Clown. It didn't take long to find a spot where he could dig a better den.

A large tree had fallen and was lying on its side propped up at an angle. Runt saw that he could dig a good den with a couple of ways in and out so they wouldn't be trapped at a single entrance. The tree branches would conceal the den and make it harder for a large animal to get to them.

It would take a lot of digging, but it would solve Runt's first problem.

Runt thought that his second problem might solve itself. When he had searched for his new den, he had gotten a lot of faint whiffs of rabbit odor. Most of the scent seemed to be coming from under the snow. Runt didn't know why the rabbits were under the snow. Maybe they slept there in the winter. Anyway, there were rabbits around, and Runt was confident that he would find a way to get at them.

It took Runt most of the day to get the new den ready. He would dig for a while and then go back to check on Clown. Finally, about mid-day Clown crawled out from the old burrow. He moved slowly in the deep snow and was limping badly, but he didn't look or smell sick. Clown followed Runt to the new den site. Runt saw that Clown limped a little less after he had walked a while, and that was probably a good thing.

Clown was very nervous about going even a short distance into the forest, but he trusted Runt. He felt a little better when he saw the almost completed den. It looked like an excellent place for two wolves out on their own.

When Runt had Clown settled in the new den he went hunting for rabbits, sure he'd be able to get one or two.

Moving quickly and sniffing in the snow it didn't take long to get the scent of a rabbit burrow under a large bush. After a short search, he was right over the burrow and started digging quickly, but when he got to it, it was empty. He was puzzled. He was sure there had been rabbits here. He looked around and realized the problem. On the other side of the bush, there were two new holes in the snow with rabbit tracks leading away from them. The rabbits had dug escape holes for their burrow just as Runt had for the new den. Runt and Clown would have no dinner that night.

It was going to be very hard for one wolf to hunt rabbits under the snow. Runt would need another plan.

For the next few days, Runt was able to catch a rabbit or other small animal from time to time, mostly by luck. He and Clown had enough food to keep them alive, but not much more. It was still early winter, and things would get more difficult as it got colder.

The good news was that Clown seemed to be getting better, but he was still too stiff and sore to be able to hunt. The couple of times he had tried, he'd been too slow to catch anything.

One afternoon when the snow had stopped, and the sun was out, Runt lay outside near the den thinking. He remembered when he and Clown had killed that deer in the high grass near Wolf Hill, and how he had led the yearlings on hunts when they had turned fleeing animals back into the rest of the pack. He wondered if something like that might work here.

Runt walked over to Clown and nudged him awake, and then led the way to a place where there were rabbits. When he got the scent of rabbit under the snow, he slowly crept forward with Clown alongside him. When they got to the spot where the scent was strongest, Runt stopped and motioned with his head for Clown to stay where he was. Then Runt circled around to a place where it was most likely for the rabbits to have their escape holes. When Runt was in position, he looked back at Clown and nodded. Clown looked confused for a moment, but then he understood what Runt was doing. Clown walked up to a spot right over the rabbit burrow and started digging. A few seconds later, a rabbit burst out of the snow just to Runt's left. Runt lunged for the rabbit but missed. The second rabbit out of the hole wasn't so lucky. Runt and Clown would have rabbit for dinner.

Over the next few days, Runt and Clown perfected their rabbit hunting technique. It didn't always work. It wasn't possible to guess exactly where the rabbits' escape holes would be, and a lot of rabbits got away. They caught enough, however, to keep themselves going, for a while at least.

The wolves would soon face a problem. The more successful they were at hunting, the fewer rabbits there would be near the den. They would have to start hunting farther and farther away, which meant they would have to work harder and harder for each rabbit they caught. Before long they would be using more energy to catch each rabbit than they got in return from their meal.

There were deer in the forest, smaller than the deer that the pack hunted on the plains, but a lot bigger than a rabbit. One deer would give them more meat than twenty rabbits, but the deer would be difficult for two wolves to catch. The deer were fast runners, and the males had large antlers that could be dangerous for a wolf. Just as bad, the deer spent most of their time farther back in the forest in places the wolves didn't know.

The deer would be getting weaker as the winter wore on and they had less to eat. But the wolves were weaker too on their diet of rabbit. Runt had to figure out how to hunt deer with just two wolves.

The first thing to do would be to explore farther into the forest, and Runt started going a little deeper into the thick trees each day. Clown was very unhappy about this, but he followed Runt whom he now thought of as his pack leader.

On a typical day, the two wolves would set off in the early morning on a scouting run into the forest. Clown was moving better now, and he could keep up with Runt at a slow lope. The wolves ran smoothly even in the deep snow, their huge paws acting like snowshoes. They would run for a while and stop to investigate whenever they caught a new scent. Runt would take them a little farther into the forest each day so they could begin to learn their way around. On the way back to the den, they would stop and hunt for the rabbits that were getting harder and harder to find.

They smelled deer almost every day and caught occasional, fleeting glimpses, but they never got close enough to even think about hunting.

Then one day on their deepest penetration into the forest they both caught a scent that brought them to an immediate stop. It was a scent they hadn't smelled in a long time.

It was the scent of another wolf.

The wolf smell was very faint, but there was no doubt that there was another wolf out there in the forest. Runt and Clown took a long time sniffing the air, trying to learn as much as they could. Was it one wolf or were there more? What was it doing? Was it dangerous?

Another wolf could be a big help — if it were friendly. A pack of wolves could be a problem if they thought that Runt and Clown were invading their territory.

The two wolves walked around trying to get a better picture of what they were smelling. They were soon pretty sure that it was just one wolf, but that raised as many questions as it answered. What was a single wolf doing out in the forest on its own? Were there others nearby? Was it scouting for prey for its pack?

After several minutes it was clear that they would have to get closer to this wolf if they were going to get more information. As usual, Runt was excited about this new adventure and Clown was nervous. The good news was that they were downwind, and the other wolf wouldn't have smelled them yet.

Runt set out with Clown staying close beside him. The two didn't go in a straight line but moved from side to side searching for more scent. The scent was getting stronger more quickly than Runt expected. The other wolf was coming toward them.

Runt decided to wait and see what this wolf would do. He and Clown went behind a small, fallen tree that would make them hard to see but wouldn't block any scent.

By now Runt had learned a lot more about the other wolf. It was definitely alone — at least for now — and it was a female. This was perhaps the strangest thing of all. Female wolves very seldom traveled on their own. Had she been forced out of a pack? If so, why? Runt got no sense that the wolf was injured or sick; what could have happened? He'd just have to wait to find out.

It wasn't long before Runt and Clown's keen ears caught the slight swish of paws moving through the snow. A moment later a wolf appeared from behind a couple of trees and came to a sudden stop. Runt saw her nose twitching, and then her head snapped, and she looked right at him.

Runt and Clown stepped out from behind the fallen tree and stood where the female could clearly see them. They were both tense, but they kept their heads and tails low to show that they were not aggressive, and they avoided looking into her eyes. Soon they saw the female's posture relax and she lowered her head and tail as well.

The three wolves stood still for a couple of minutes, and then the female raised her tail and slowly moved it from side to side. This was an invitation to come and meet her.

Runt and Clown moved close keeping their heads and tails down. They went right to the female's rear end to a spot where there are glands up under a wolf's tail that hold many of the wolf's hormones. The scent of these hormones can tell another wolf a lot. Angry and aggressive or calm and relaxed? Male or female? Sick or healthy?

After a quick check, Runt and Clown determined that this wolf was no threat, so they did the polite thing. They stood back and let her sniff them. When she finished the three stood looking at each other. The female looked a lot like Runt. She was a yearling in her second winter like him, and she was on the small side. Her fur was clean and shiny, which meant that she'd been eating, but she was thin like Runt and Clown so she'd probably been having the same problems they had getting food.

After everyone was satisfied with the initial examination, they began to sniff each other all over to learn as much as they could and to imprint the other wolves' scents in their brains.

The last thing they all did was to sniff each other at the muzzle and nose. This was a sign of trust because a wolf wouldn't let another wolf close to its face unless it was safe. When Runt and Clown sniffed the female's mouth, they found the most wonderful thing.

She had the sweetest breath they'd ever smelled.

Gunny awoke with a start. Sweetbreath! He remembered the first time he had smelled her breath. The memories were vague and cloudy, but there was no doubt about Sweetbreath. Thinking about her made him feel ... warm, good.

Gunny knew that this wasn't a dream anymore. Deep inside he knew that Sweetbreath was real. That meant that Runt and Clown were real too. He didn't understand any of these things, but he knew.

Gunny rolled over to go back to sleep. He needed to remember what happened next to Runt, Clown, and Sweetbreath.

As he fell back into sleep, his dream changed. He was no longer Runt.

He was Sweetbreath.

Sweetbreath had been looking for other wolves ever since Mother had died one moon-change ago. She needed help, but the idea of meeting strange wolves scared her. She was young, and the only wolves she had known were the wolves in her pack, and that hadn't worked out very well.

When she saw the two males step out from behind the fallen tree, her first impulse had been to turn and run. She was glad that she had waited long enough to understand that they meant her no harm. When they had finished their introductions, she knew that she would join their small pack if they would have her. They were just the type of wolf she was looking for, except ....

Phew! Their breath!

Sweetbreath's pack were forest wolves. Their forest was across a sea of grass from this forest. To get there, a wolf would have to run in a straight line for three days keeping the place where the sun comes up on her left side. Her pack hunted the deer in the forest, and she had learned how that was done.

Like Runt, Sweetbreath was different from other wolves. She was curious and adventurous and seemed fearless. The other wolves in her pack hadn't been sure what to make of her, but she was on her way to learning how to be an adult wolf.

But her pack was falling apart around her.

Wolf packs are like human societies — some work better than others, some have good luck, and some have bad luck. It's not unusual for a wolf pack to break up, sometimes forming two or more smaller packs and sometimes just dissolving into a ragged collection of individuals that go their own way.

Sweetbreath's pack had two problems — bad luck and poor leadership. The pack's Mother wolf had only two puppies in her last litter, Sweetbreath and a little male who only lived for a few days. That spring the pack leader was killed in a hunt, and there was no wolf ready to take over. This led to fights and squabbles between several wolves who thought that they should be the leader. In the meantime, no one wolf took responsibility for organizing the hunts and ensuring that the pack was fed. Even worse, with all of the turmoil, none of the wolves mated, so there had been no puppies this year.

Mother tried to help organize the hunts and set an example for the other wolves on how to act, but she was ignored. Sweetbreath watched the constant fighting and thought it was crazy. The males only cared about trying to prove how strong they were. None of them seemed to understand the other qualities needed to be a leader.

As the youngest wolf, Sweetbreath had to learn many things to be able to survive as an adult wolf. She knew that the only wolf that would take the time to teach her was Mother. Sweetbreath spent most of her time with Mother, watching and learning. They would often hunt small animals together, and Mother taught her how two wolves could work together to catch rabbits that were hiding under the snow.

Two wolves could not hunt deer. It took at least three and even then it was dangerous. The male deer had large antlers, and all of the deer had sharp hooves. One kick from a deer could break a wolf's jaw, which would mean a slow, painful death by starvation. Sweetbreath's pack had always hunted deer together, and they were often successful. But without a strong leader more and more of their hunts were coming up empty. Not all of the wolves were as good at hunting rabbits and other small animals as Mother and Sweetbreath, and none of the wolves were inclined to share when they did make a kill.

The situation was becoming desperate when the pack had a bit of good luck. On a loosely-organized hunt, they stumbled across a small deer herd. When the pack gave chase, one of the deer lagged far behind the others. It was injured, and the wolves were able to make a quick kill. This was the most food the wolves had seen in a long time, but it wasn't enough for every wolf to eat its fill.

In a well-run pack, the leaders would have eaten first but left enough for all of the wolves to get a share. But here, with no real leadership, it was every wolf for itself. When Mother and Sweetbreath tried to get in for a share of the food they were driven away by several snarling, snapping males. Mother might have been seriously hurt, but Sweetbreath charged in, and the other wolves backed off. They were more interested in eating than fighting.

After this, Mother and Sweetbreath knew that their time with the pack was coming to an end. As far as the adult males were concerned, they were just two more mouths competing for food. They would be driven out, and, possibly, injured or killed.

It was time to go.

One afternoon in early winter, while the wolves were resting in the sun, Mother and Sweetbreath just got up and walked away. No one seemed to notice or care.

Mother led the way with the place where the sun comes up on their right side. As far as Sweetbreath was concerned, one direction was as good as another and she followed along. Sweetbreath had never been outside the forest in her life, but now they must leave the pack's home territory.

Mother was in no hurry. The pack was too disorganized to come after them. They could take their time and hunt along the way. They should have a better chance of finding small animals the farther away they got from the pack.

Mother had another reason for going slowly. There were many things she had to teach Sweetbreath, and her time was growing short. She had not been feeling well for some time, and she had no appetite. Most wolves didn't live more than five years, and Mother was seven now. It was time for her to go, but she didn't want to leave until Sweetbreath was ready to survive on her own.

It took three days to reach the end of the forest which was also the end of the pack's territory. Every step of the way Mother tried to show Sweetbreath something new — new food sources, new places to find shelter, and, most importantly, new dangers. One day the two of them came across fresh tracks in the snow, the largest tracks Sweetbreath had ever seen. Mother let Sweetbreath smell the tracks and then shook her head to tell her that this was an animal they had to avoid. Sweetbreath took a long time smelling the tracks to make sure she would remember this scent.

When they came to the edge of the forest and looked out at the endless snow-covered plain stretching before them, Sweetbreath wanted to turn and run back into the trees. She had never imagined that there could be a place with no trees, and where you could see for so far. When she turned to look at Mother, she saw her looking back toward their home with a sad expression. That was when Sweetbreath understood that Mother was dying, and she would never see her beloved forest again.

They pushed on for three more days. Sweetbreath didn't think that there could be any other animals out here in the snowy waste, but she soon learned that she was wrong. There were mice and rabbits and other small animals, just as there had been in the forest, and they were able to eat enough to keep them going. Other animals were far too big for two wolves to hunt, and they were best avoided. At night when they had to find shelter, Mother showed Sweetbreath the long grass that lay flat under the weight of snow. It only took a little digging to get down to where they had a warm burrow insulated by both snow and grass.

When they came out of their den the next morning, Sweetbreath could see that Mother was very ill. Sweetbreath wanted Mother to stay in their burrow while she went out to hunt, but Mother insisted on continuing. Mother seemed to think that there was something ahead, something she must reach. Sweetbreath was able to catch a small rabbit, but Mother wouldn't eat.

They moved as quickly as they could even though Sweetbreath could see that Mother was in pain. At midday, they stopped to rest, and Sweetbreath climbed a small hill to check for scent. There was a slight breeze blowing down from ahead, and it brought with it a familiar odor. It was so familiar that Sweetbreath hadn't paid attention to it, but now she knew why Mother insisted on pushing them on.

It was the scent of trees. There was a forest ahead.

Shortly before dark, they stood at the edge of the forest. It looked very much like the place where Sweetbreath had lived her whole life. She saw that Mother's condition was worse, but her eyes were gleaming with joy. Despite her pain, Mother made Sweetbreath go farther into the woods until the vast, empty plains were no longer in sight. Then Mother lay down, while Sweetbreath dug their hole for the night.

When they were settled in their burrow curled up together, Mother licked Sweetbreath's muzzle for a long time.

She's saying goodbye Sweetbreath thought.

The next morning Mother lay still, not moving or breathing. When Sweetbreath looked at her, she saw that the expression on Mother's face was peaceful. She had died in the forest, and she had done everything she could to teach Sweetbreath how to be a good wolf.

Sweetbreath left Mother in the den and covered it with snow. When she was finished, she sat for a few minutes looking down. She was lonely and a little scared, but she was excited, too.

I'm on my own, but, thanks to Mother, I'm in the forest, and I know what I need to do. I think I can make it.

But it sure would be better if I can find some other wolves.

Sweeetbreath looked at the two males. One was a full-grown adult, and the other was a yearling like her. She was surprised to see that the young wolf, who had probably been the runt of his litter, seemed to be the leader. The other wolf was just standing there waiting to see what he would do. She was waiting too. Would he accept her, or try to chase her away?

Her question was answered a minute later when Runt moved alongside, and, with a gentle bump on her shoulder, indicated that she should follow them.

Runt and Clown turned and began to trot back toward their den. Sweetbreath didn't hesitate. She followed right behind them.

In the next few days, the wolves learned about each other. They realized that three wolves could have much better success hunting small animals than one or two by themselves. Sweetbreath saw that their way of hunting rabbits was the same that Mother had taught her. Runt and Clown were happy to see that Sweetbreath knew her way around in the forest much better than they did. She knew about more animals and how to hunt them.

After three days together, the three of them lay down in their burrow with full bellies for the first time in a long while.

Usually, male and female wolves didn't den together, but they decided that was something they could worry about when the snow was gone. They spent half a day digging to enlarge their burrow and then moved in together.

Sweetbreath was happy with her new situation except for one thing that she set out to fix the next day.

Runt and Clown were puzzled by what Sweetbreath was doing the next morning. She was nosing all over the area near their burrow, but she didn't seem to be hunting. She would sniff and then paw at the snow and then move a short distance and do it again. Finally, they saw her tail go up in excitement, and she started digging furiously. After a minute or two they could see that she was tugging on something under the snow with her teeth. She pulled out three things that looked like strange sticks and brought them over. Then she lay down and started gnawing on one.

The other two wolves had no idea what Sweetbreath was doing. After she had chewed on the stick for a while, she picked it up and held it under Runt's nose. Runt was surprised that this strange stick smelled like her breath. He leaned down and sniffed one of the other sticks, and then picked it up and started chewing. It was tough and had a stringy texture. It felt good to chew, and it had a sweet taste.

Later Runt and Clown would learn that these weren't sticks but the roots of a forest plant. The wolves of Sweetbreath's pack had found these roots generations ago and often would spend many lazy hours just relaxing and chewing.

Sweetbreath was happy to see that Runt and Clown enjoyed chewing the roots. This was going to make living with them in the burrow a lot more pleasant.

Now that they were eating better, Clown's leg seemed to be improving every day. Before long, Sweetbreath started taking him and Runt on hunts farther into the woods than they had gone before.

The deeper into the woods they went, the more deer they saw. As the winter moved into the coldest part of the year, they were able to get closer and closer to the herds of deer who were being weakened by having to dig through deep snow to get a few bites of forage.

Finally, Sweetbreath decided that it was time to hunt deer. Although she had accepted Runt as her pack leader, she knew more about this type of hunting than he did. Runt was happy to let her take charge.

With Sweetbreath in front, the three wolves loped into the forest with their noses working hard sniffing for deer scent. Sweetbreath was able to find the places where the snow was the firmest so that they could run almost effortlessly. It wasn't long before she got the first scent of deer. She immediately turned to keep the three of them downwind and slowed so that they could approach quietly. Soon they were just creeping along, moving carefully and quietly. They couldn't see the deer yet, but they knew they were close.

When she found a good hiding place in a small stand of pines, Sweetbreath stopped. With a nod of her head, she told Runt and Clown to stay there, and she left, going quietly back the way they had come.

Runt saw that she was going to circle around and drive the deer toward him and Clown. It was just like the deer that the two of them had killed when they were still with the pack, except this time they were hunting a whole herd.

Sweetbreath had never done this before. She had watched older wolves from her pack and knew what she had to do. But when her pack hunted, there were always three or four wolves to drive the deer, not just one young female, and, there was a whole pack of wolves waiting for the herd of fleeing deer, not just two. She tried not to think about any of that.

When she got to where they had turned downwind, she went in the opposite direction to get upwind of the herd. The deer were now off to her right and far enough away not to scent her. She hoped.

When she thought she had gone far enough, she turned to her right. She planned to come out upwind of the herd, but if she was wrong about exactly where the deer were and came in below them, she could spook them in the wrong direction. She couldn't see the deer or smell them, all she could do was follow her instincts about where she thought they would be.

She moved slowly now so the deer wouldn't see her too soon. Creeping along she began to see glimpses of color through the trees. The deer were right where she thought. Now she just had to get them to run in the direction she wanted.

Moving slowly and quietly, she got close enough that she could begin to see individual deer. There were several bucks with large spreads of antlers. If they decided to fight instead of run, she could be in trouble. Somehow she had to convince them to run.

She got as close as she could to the deer and stopped. She would wait for them to get her scent. In a minute a light breeze moved through the trees, and she saw one of the bucks raise its head and look right at her. She was close enough to see his eyes go wide in fright.

Now!

She threw her head back and made a sound that every creature in the forest had feared for thousands of years — the howl of a wolf on the hunt — then she charged right at the nearest buck snarling and snapping her teeth.

The buck didn't stop to wonder why he'd only heard one wolf howling. He turned and ran, and the rest of the herd followed him going straight downwind, right to where Runt and Clown were waiting.

Sweetbreath howled again and ran after the deer making as much noise as she could. Now it was up to the boys.

Runt and Clown heard Sweetbreath's howl and knew what was happening. In only a moment they heard the deer running toward them. Runt had never been in a situation like this before, and he wasn't sure what to do. There were only two of them, and those deer were big and moving fast. Then he looked at Clown.

Clown had moved forward a few steps and was standing calmly watching as the herd came closer. He'd been on more hunts than Runt, and he knew what he had to do.

When the deer came into sight, they weren't bunched tightly. If they had been, it would have been impossible for two wolves to separate one of them out. Instead, they had been caught so much by surprise that they were loosely scattered in ones and twos. Clown's eyes scanned the herd and found what he was looking for. A large doe that was running just a little slower than the others, limping just a bit on a hind leg. Clown moved quickly to get between her and the rest of the herd. Runt followed.

By the time Sweetbreath found them, the doe was down, and Clown was finishing her off with a bite to the throat.

The three wolves now had more meat than any of them had seen in months, and they began to eat. When they had eaten as much as they could hold, they lay down next to the deer panting. There was still a lot of meat left. As soon as they had rested, they would have to dig a temporary den so they could stay close and protect their kill from the jackals and others that would try to steal it.

But for now, it was enough to know that they would be able to eat well for at least a few days.

Gunny came awake slowly. The memory of that first hunt with Sweetbreath was as real as one of his memories of searching with The Man. He didn't know how this was possible, and he didn't know how he could be both Runt and Sweetbreath, but he didn't have to know. Sweetbreath, Runt, and Clown were as real as The Man, Mom, and The Boy. It was all very strange, but he didn't care. These were good memories, and he was enjoying them. That was all that mattered.

CHAPTER SEVEN

Vision

OLDEST BOY HEARD THE WOLVES CALLING TO HIM every night. It wasn't frightening, but it bothered him because he didn't understand what it meant. He had to talk to someone.

When he told his parents, his mother just laughed and told him it was only a boy's dream. His father looked worried.

"Oldest Boy, we will wait one hand of nights, to see if you keep hearing these wolves. Come and talk with us then, and we will decide what to do."

"Yes, Father."

After the fifth night, he went back to his parents.

"Father, Mother, the wolves are still calling, and their call is getting louder."

His mother again tried to tell him that it was just a silly dream, but his father held up his hand to quiet her. "Oldest Boy, I believe that you hear something. It may be wolves, or it may not be. Your Mother and I are not wise enough to know. You must tell your story to Chief and Wise Mother. I will speak to them first."

Two days later, Oldest Boy was summoned to Chief's hut. When he arrived, he saw Chief and Wise Mother sitting around a small fire of fragrant pine wood.

"Chief, Wise Mother, you want to see me?"

"Yes, Oldest Boy, sit," Chief commanded, "Tell us of your dreams."

"Every night I hear the wolves, and they are calling to me."

"What do you mean?" Wise Mother asked, "Do you hear them howling?"

"No, it is as if they are speaking to me. I don't understand the words, but I understand what they want."

"Do you hear them with your ears?" Wise Mother asked.

"No, it is as if they are in my head and talking to me, but they use sounds I have never heard before."

"And what do you think they are saying?" Chief asked.

"When they are talking to me my mind keeps saying one word, over and over. My mind is saying, 'Come.'"

"What do you think this means, Oldest Boy?" Wise Mother asked.

"Just as we are searching for the wolves, I think the wolves are searching for us. They want me to find them."

"Why do you think the wolves are talking to you and not one of our scouts or hunters?" Chief asked, "Why do they want a boy to find them?"

"I don't know, Chief. I can only tell you what I hear."

"Very well. Wise Mother and I will talk. Come and see us tomorrow and we will tell you what we think."

"Thank you, Chief. Thank you, Wise Mother."

The next day Oldest Boy went to the Chief's hut and found him and Wise Mother just as before. They looked as if they had not moved since he last saw them. As soon as he sat, Chief began to speak.

"Wise Mother and I have thought and spoken, and we believe that your dream is real. We think that this is something that affects all of The People, so we must tell all of The People. Tonight, the moon will be full. After Memory tells her story, we will tell The People of your dream."

"What will I have to do?"

"Tonight, you will learn."

Oldest Boy had always loved the stories Memory told and listened to every word, but this night was different. While she was speaking, all he could think of was what Chief and Wise Mother would say to The People about him. When Memory had finished speaking, he could not remember anything she'd said.

Finally, Chief rose and stood before the fire. There were no secrets among The People. The group was too small and lived too closely together. Everyone knew that Oldest Boy had been having dreams about the wolves, but no one knew what Chief and Wise Mother had decided about these dreams. The People were almost as anxious about what Chief would say as Oldest Boy.

"You all know the Wolf Story," Chief began, "You know that many, many moon-changes ago it was the Oldest Boy who had the idea how The People could hunt with the wolves. Now, it seems that this Oldest Boy here has been chosen to help The People find the wolves again.

"Wise Mother and I believe that Oldest Boy has had a Vision."

Chief stood quietly while The People talked excitedly. A Vision was very rare. No one could remember the last time a Chief had said that one of The People had a Vision.

"Oldest Boy's Vision is that the wolves are calling to him. Wise Mother and I believe that this is true. We believe that this is a Quest Vision."

The People gasped in surprise. A Quest Vision! This was a thing of legend. Memory told a story about a Quest Vision, but the story was so old that it had become vague and hard to understand. What could this mean?

Chief continued, "A Quest Vision asks for a Quest. The word, 'asks,' is very important. The Vision does not demand a Quest. A Quest is very dangerous. The person who receives the Quest Vision is the only one who can decide whether or not to go.

"Before I ask Oldest Boy if he will accept this Quest, we will talk. Who wants to speak?"

First Hunter stood. He was the oldest and most experienced of all of the hunters.

"Chief, why did Oldest Boy have this Vision? Why not a hunter or a scout? We would have a much better chance of finding the wolves than a boy."

"Oldest Boy was chosen. I don't know why. I don't know where this Vision came from. All Wise Mother and I know is that it is true."

Oldest Boy's mother stood next, "Why will this Quest be so dangerous for my son. What must he do?"

"Mother, a Quest is for one person and one person only. Your son must go alone. We don't know where he must go. The Vision will guide him."

"But he is just a boy! He doesn't know how to ... to ...," Mother sank to her knees sobbing.

"Oldest Boy's Mother is right. Oldest Boy has much to learn. We have one more moon-change of winter cold. The Quest must begin as soon as enough snow has melted. First Hunter and First Scout you will have one moon-change to teach Oldest Boy all your skills; how to track, how to hunt for food, how to defend himself. First Cooker, you must teach Oldest Boy all the tricks of fire and how to cook and how to find good plants to eat. First Toolmaker, you will make sure that Oldest Boy has the best knife, the best spear, the best bow and arrows you can make.

"I say to all of The People that the most important thing we can do for the next moon-change is to help Oldest Boy prepare for his Quest.

"If, that is, he chooses to go. Oldest Boy, come here beside me."

When Oldest Boy stood next to Chief in front of the fire, Chief spoke, "Oldest Boy, you have had a true Vision, and this Vision asks for a Quest. This Quest will be hard and dangerous. You do not have to accept, and if you do not, no one will think less of you because we know that you did not ask for this. What do you say?"

While Chief had been talking, Oldest Boy had been thinking, but not of danger or hardships, but of wolves.

I will find the wolves! He thought.

"Yes, Chief, I will go. I will go gladly!"

"Very well. Your name is no longer Oldest Boy.

"Your name is Wolf Finder."

All of The People had to be able to help with the hunt. That was how they got most of their food. Since he had first begun to walk, Wolf Finder had been learning about hunting and scouting, and he thought that he knew a lot. The first day he spent with First Hunter and First Scout he found out how little he really knew.

He learned that what he had done so far on his hunts — going along with a group of The People to help kill the animals that the hunters and scouts had found — was a lot different than finding these animals and bringing them to bay himself, let alone actually killing them on his own.

The first advice he got was to become very good at hunting rabbits, squirrels, and other small animals. It would be a lot easier, and safer, than trying to kill a deer or a bison calf on his own.

First Hunter quizzed him on tracks. Wolf Finder knew most of the animal tracks, but there were two that he had never seen.

"I will test you on these tracks every day until you leave," First Hunter said, "Because they are the most important and because you have never seen them. This is a wolf track."

First Hunter drew the wolf track with its large center pad with two rounded points, four toe pads, and four claw marks in the snow. He showed Wolf Finder how these tracks would look when they were fresh and when they were old and when they were on dry ground, mud or snow.

"You have never seen these tracks because the wolves left when you were a baby. You must know them. This is the whole reason you are going on this Quest."

He then drew another track with an oddly-shaped center pad with three rounded points, four toe points with one toe out farther than the others, and no claw marks. Wolf Finder recognized it immediately.

"That is the track of Little Cat," he said.

"Correct. Now, look at this track."

First Hunter drew a track that was the same as Little Cat, but many times larger. Wolf Finder could fit his hand inside it with almost enough room for another hand.

"This is another track you must know. This is an animal that you must avoid, the most dangerous animal in the forest. This is the Big Cat. Big Cat can move as quietly as a whisper and can kill an adult bison with one bite to its neck. Fortunately, there are not too many of them, and they hunt alone, not in a pack like the wolves and us. If you see any sign of Big Cat, you must get away as fast as you can."

First Scout showed him how to use the stars and sun to tell direction. She taught him how to make signs on trees and build small piles of stone to mark his trail so he could find his way home. She told him to keep track of hills and streams because these would be good landmarks.

Wolf Finder thought that he could spend all the time he had before he left with the hunters and scouts, but there were many more things to learn.

First Toolmaker told him that he would make him the best tools, but that these would be no good unless he knew how to use them and take care of them. He spent hours learning to sharpen a knife and spear and string a bow. First Hunter told him that he would only have one chance to make a kill and his spear or arrow must always fly true. With First Toolmaker he spent more hours learning how to throw a spear and shoot an arrow like a seasoned hunter.

Then he dug in the snow so that First Cooker could show him how to find the plants he would need. First Cooker showed him how to use the stomach of a deer to boil water, and which leaves he could use to make a hot drink that would make him feel better when he was tired. He learned which plants he could eat and which ones to boil and drink if he was sick or make into a paste to stop bleeding or to ease pain. He also learned how to make a fire in any weather with wet wood or dry wood or leaves or anything he could find.

Every night he would go exhausted back to his cave to find presents from The People. Good boots made from soft deerskin, a robe for sleeping in that was made from the fur of ermine that was warm but very light, and many other things.

Then one morning just after the full moon he walked out of his cave, and with one sniff of the warm air, he could tell that it would soon be time to go. The snow was melting, and the sun was staying in the sky longer. More importantly, the call of the wolves was louder than ever.

For the next two days, The People worked to prepare a feast. The day after the feast, Wolf Finder would leave. Although he had many things to do, Memory told him that she must have one day with him to learn his story. For hour after hour, she worked to learn everything she could about him. She would ask a question, close her eyes while he answered, and then keep her eyes shut for a long time while she memorized his answer, then ask another question.

At the feast, everyone told him how proud they were, and how happy that he would be bringing back the wolves. They gave him more gifts, and he ate more food than he ever had.

Finally, it was time. He stood on the trail leading off into the forest and looked back at his home and The People, his people. Suddenly, he felt very young and very scared.

What am I doing? I'm just a boy. I can't survive on my own in the forest. I'll never find the wolves. I'll die.

He found that he was shivering and not from the cold. He took a deep breath and closed his eyes. For the first time, he could hear the wolves calling while he was awake. He remembered Chief saying that the Vision would guide him.

I will trust the Vision and the wolves. They will guide me and keep me safe. I will find them and bring them to The People. I will.

With a last glance back and a wave to his mother, he turned and walked down the trail.

CHAPTER EIGHT

Wolf to Dog

CLAY WAS UNUSUALLY QUIET AT BREAKFAST. His dream the night before had been so vivid and real and full of details that he couldn't stop thinking about it. It had been so real that he was pretty sure that if he had a flint spearhead and a flaking stone he would know how to sharpen the edge.

He really wanted to talk to someone about it, but he wasn't ready yet. He didn't know if he could explain it well enough that whoever he told wouldn't think he was crazy. He decided to keep talking with Coop to try to learn more about wolves and dogs and maybe a little bit about how people lived back in those days.

After breakfast, he followed Coop and the rest of his family out to the living room. He was relieved when Coop opened the discussion.

"So, Clay, you want to know how a wolf became a dog. What else?"

"I've been thinkin' about the story you told about the boy who found the wolf, and I'd like to know more about what it was like to live back then."

"OK, let's talk about how a wolf might have become a dog, and we'll see how much time we have later for your second question."

"Great, thanks!"

"First of all, we have to define what we mean when we say that a wolf became a dog. What does that mean? If we look at a picture of a wolf alongside a picture of a dog, we can see a lot of differences. Dogs are generally smaller and have shorter legs and muzzles. Their heads are smaller, which means that their brains are smaller, too.

"Of course, the most significant differences are in behavior or personality. Dogs do things that wolves never do. Here's an example: what does Gunny do when you point to something or look at something?"

"Uh … I'm not sure."

"Try it. Get Gunny's attention and point to something here in the room, anything."

Clay said, "Gunny," and when Gunny lifted his head, Clay pointed at a bookcase on the other side of the room. Gunny's eyes and head followed the movement of Clay's hand, and, when it stopped, Gunny was looking right at the bookcase.

"Wow, he looked right where I was pointing. I guess I knew he did that but never paid any attention to it."

"Right, most people don't understand how amazing that is. Dogs pay attention to us and follow our gestures. Wolves don't do that, and even our closest animal relative, the chimpanzee, doesn't do that. That means that there's something in the dog's brain that is different from almost every other animal, and we're starting to think that it's that kind of difference that made it possible for some wolves to join up with humans and eventually evolve into dogs."

"I've got another example for you," Sam said.

"What's that, Sam?" Coop asked.

"Clay, you've watched me and Gunny doing our search and rescue training. What did you see?"

"Uh …. well, ….Oh yeah, I got it. You would start walkin' back and forth across the area you were searchin', and Gunny would sorta follow you, but he'd go off in different directions lookin' for odor and then come back and check in on you. Then, when he found somethin', he'd sit and bark to let you know where it was."

"Very good."

"Sam, that's a great example. I'm sure it took a lot of training to get Gunny to do all that, but you could never train a wolf to do it, never, or any other animal for that matter. Dogs are just different.

"That doesn't mean that being a wolf is a bad thing. Wolves are very social animals who cooperate together in everything they do from hunting to rearing their young. It's this sociability that we think made wolves the primary candidate for becoming our first partner.

"As I said before, we now think that certain wolves, wolves with genetic mutations that made them less fearful of new things, domesticated themselves."

"I don't understand," Clay said, "What does that mean? Why would a wolf domesticate itself?"

"Think about it. Imagine you're a wolf living fifteen thousand years ago. Times are tough. Every day is a struggle for survival. Then one day you run into a group of new animals that walk on two legs and have so much food that they throw some of it away. You watch these animals and see that they're good hunters. They have things that you don't understand, bows and arrows and spears that let them kill their prey while it's still too far away to be dangerous to them. Sometimes they kill more animals than they can eat or carry away, and you learn that following them around is an excellent way to get free food.

"At the same time, the two legs are figuring out that you and the rest of your pack are better at finding and chasing down prey than they are. Then some smart human comes up with an idea about how to hunt together with you and the other wolves.

"Here's how it might have worked. One day you and the rest of the pack are out hunting bison, and you realize that a band of the two-legged animals is trotting along behind you. After a while, you find a small herd of bison and start after them, and the two-legs keep following you. You chase the bison for a couple of miles until they get tired and stop and form a defensive circle. Now you're faced with an angry bunch of large animals with giant horns, and you know it's gonna be very dangerous for your pack to try to break into that circle and separate out one of the bison that you might be able to kill.

"Then along come the two-legs, and they don't even slow down. They run right up to the bison and start shooting arrows and throwing spears. Before you know it, they've killed two or three bison and chased the rest away. You sit and watch while the two-legs butcher the bison and walk away with as much meat as they can carry, leaving the rest of the meat for your pack. There's more food than you've seen in a long time.

"It doesn't take you and the other wolves long to figure out that hanging around with these new animals is a good deal.

"From the human's viewpoint, it makes a lot of sense to let the wolf pack do all the hard work of finding and chasing down the prey so that they can just walk up and make the kill.

"It's a win-win for everyone."

"Except the bison," Clay said.

"Well, yeah. When a band of humans started working together with a pack of wolves, things got pretty tough for the prey animals."

What Coop's saying sounds just like what that Oldest Boy told The People to do to hunt with the wolves. But I dreamed that two nights ago. How could I have known that?

"Now," Coop continued, "Let's imagine that you're a wolf who's a little different from the rest. You've been born with a genetic mutation that makes you a little less fearful, a little more adventurous than your average wolf.

"You're a wolf that's on its way to becoming a dog. You're a wolfdog.

"When the hunt was over most of the wolves went back to the den site and hung out with their buddies. But you follow the humans back to where they live in a couple of caves. You watch the humans and what they do. You learn about fire and figure out that you don't have to be afraid of it. You realize that the human pack is a lot like a wolf pack. These two-legged animals all share the meat from the hunt, and everyone helps to take care of the two-legged puppies.

"And then one day our wolfdog, you, meets one of the humans up close."

"Like that story, you told me about the boy and the wolf who killed that rabbit."

"Exactly. However it happened, both the wolfdog and the human saw some advantage in being together and made a pact to cooperate with each other.

"Like I said before, it's been the most successful partnership in the history of the world."

"But it's still a partnership between wolves and us. Where do the dogs come in?"

"Boy, you're not gonna let me off easy are you, Clay?

"OK, remember we're talking about a wolfdog. Something that's already started to become different from a wild wolf. Maybe that genetic modification that's made the wolfdog less fearful has also made it better at paying attention to what a human does."

"Like following our hands when we point?"

"Exactly. Maybe not as good as Gunny, but a start along the way."

"It took years and years for the wolfdogs that first began to live with humans to change into something we might recognize as a dog. On the other hand, it happened a lot faster than we used to think it could.

"The wolfdog that started living with and hunting with humans generally got more food and lived a safer life than his wild brothers and sisters."

"Why was he safer?"

"Not many large predators would choose to come after a band of humans with spears and arrows and fire. A wolfdog who could live near the fire circle would be a lot safer, not to mention warmer, than one living out in the wild. In turn, the wolfdog, with his excellent hearing and sense of smell could warn the humans whenever any dangerous animals came close. Again, it was a win-win.

"Eating more and being safer, these wolfdogs had a better chance to pass their genes along to their offspring. A lot of the puppies of these wolfdogs inherited what we might call the dog genes. I'm pretty sure that people fifteen thousand years ago thought that puppies are just as cute as we think they are today. These puppies grew up playing with human kids and learning how to live with humans. At the same time, their parents would be teaching them how to be wolves."

"Those are the wolves that eventually became dogs?"

"Exactly, Clay. And it really didn't take too long.

"The tamest puppies, the ones who had no fear of people and fire and the other strange things that come along with living with humans, grew up living longer than their wild brothers and sisters. Some of the puppies, the ones who didn't inherit the dog genes, drifted away back to the wild wolves, but the ones who stayed got a little tamer with each new generation.

"Now comes the strange part that we paleontologists don't understand very well. It turns out that when you breed a dog, or any animal, for one, specific thing, like tameness, you tend to get puppies that are tamer, but you also get other changes as well."

"Like what?"

"In the case of our wolfdogs you started to get puppies with floppy ears, and shorter muzzles and shorter legs for example."

"Why?"

"We're not really sure, but it happens all the time, and it only takes a few generations, maybe fifteen or twenty years. I know that seems like a long time to you, but when you're talking about things that happened fifteen thousand years ago, it's hardly anything."

"Wolves and humans partnered up fifteen thousand years ago because they both thought there was something in it for them, and then some wolves stayed with the humans instead of going back to the wolf pack, and those wolves eventually became dogs. Is that it?"

"That's it exactly. Very good, Clay."

"That means that Gunny's great, great, great, something grandfather was a wolf."

"Yep."

Clay looked over at where Gunny was sleeping near Grandpa, smiled and said, "Wow, Gunny, I don't know if I feel safe having you sleeping in my room. What if you forget you're a dog and attack me in the middle of the night?"

Gunny lifted his head and smiled back, and then put his head down and went back to sleep.

"OK, one more question."

"Wow, Clay, you are a curious kid," Coop said.

"Yeah, in more ways than one," Mike said.

"Thanks, Dad."

"What's your question?" Coop asked.

"You said a couple of times that the dog and human partnership was the most successful one ever. What does that mean?"

"Let's say humans and wolves got together about fifteen thousand years ago, and the wolves started evolving into dogs. What happened next?"

"I don't know."

"A couple thousand years later, a blink of an eye in evolutionary terms, humans have domesticated sheep and cattle — something they couldn't have done without help from dogs for herding and guarding the animals — and they've started to live in villages so they could care for their animals instead of roaming around following the prey animals. Once they settled into a village, they began to plant crops. Next thing you know, we've got farms and cities and Google. If it weren't for dogs, we'd either still be nomadic hunter-gatherers or our race would be extinct.

"Today there are over seven billion members of our species on the planet and almost a billion dogs. I'd say that's pretty successful, wouldn't you?"

"Wow!"

"So, what about my other question, what was it like to be a boy way back then?"

"That's not exactly a simple question. 'Way back then,' in what we call the Upper Pleistocene, a lot of things were changing. The Neanderthals, who, by the way, were bigger, stronger, and possibly even smarter than us, had already died off, and modern humans, people like us, were taking over. The climate was changing, the landscape was changing. Pretty much everything was changing, so when you talk about what it was like to be a boy back then the answer is, 'It depends.' It depends on where you were, and what tribe or group you belonged to and a lot of other things."

Coop was interrupted when Clay's Mom walked into the room. "OK, everyone, beach time!"

"Awww, Mom, we're busy talkin'."

"You can talk anytime. We've got a beautiful day outside, and we're gonna go enjoy it. No arguments, get movin'."

Clay sighed, "Yes, Ma'am."

"It's OK, Clay. We'll try to finish this before I leave tomorrow," Coop said.

As usual, Mom had been right. It was the best day of their vacation. The kids spent most of the day on the beach with just a few breaks for something to eat and drink. The adults took turns supervising.

Clay hoped that he'd have a chance to talk some more with Coop, but it didn't work out. After dinner, the whole family played wild games of Mexican Train making up the rules as they went along so that all eleven of them could play a game designed for six. It was a lot of fun, and Clay understood that he couldn't take up all of Coop's time.

Still, he was disappointed.

That night Gunny followed him up to bed again.

I wonder if these strange dreams have something to do with Gunny being in my room.

Gunny was asleep before Clay turned the light out.

Clay thought that he would lie awake thinking about all the things Coop had been telling him, but he quickly drifted off.

And began remembering.

CHAPTER NINE

Quest

IN THE PART OF THE FOREST WHERE THE PEOPLE LIVED the trees were scattered, and there were many clearings. There were hills and streams and not much heavy brush. It was good hunting land, which is why the people lived there. Wolf Finder knew the land was like this for one day's walk toward the Place Where the Sun Goes at Night. That was as far as he had ever gone. First Scout had told him that in three days walk the forest would become thicker with the trees closer together and fewer clearings. She couldn't tell him more than that because the hunters and scouts had not gone farther than that away from The People's home. He thought he might have to go much farther than that. He didn't know why he felt that. Maybe it was the Vision speaking to him.

He was carrying everything he owned. He had a pouch filled with dried meat, berries, and fat, but this was for emergencies. He expected to feed himself by hunting and gathering plants. He had his ermine robe, and a coat cut from a bison hide rolled up inside a sleeping mat made from tightly-woven fiber. He was wearing all his other clothes. He had another pouch with flints and tinder for making fire, and a third with small, hard rocks for sharpening his spear and knife. A fourth pouch had smaller pouches inside. Each small pouch had dried plants that he would use if he was tired, or hurt, in pain, or to stop bleeding. His deer stomach was folded into this pouch.

His knife was made of flint and so sharp that he had to be careful not to cut himself. The blade was set in a piece of bone from the leg of a bison that First Toolmaker had carved into the shape of a wolf. He didn't know how First Toolmaker had carved the bone so that it not only looked like a wolf, but it also fit his hand perfectly. The same was true of his spear thrower, a stick about as long as his arm with a cup on one end and the wolf handle on the other. By fitting the butt of his spear into the cup of the spear thrower, he could throw his spear with much more force. The spear with its thrower was his weapon for taking down larger animals. The flint blade of the spear was more than twice the size of his knife and just as sharp. He also had a bow and some arrows with bone tips. These would be used for small animals like rabbits and squirrels.

Wolf Finder had never seen a wolf, but he knew what one looked like. His father was Artist. He drew pictures on the walls of the caves and on pieces of hide. Like Memory's stories, his pictures told about the things The People had done.

Wolf Finder's prize possession was a wooden carving of a wolf made by his father. It hung around his neck on a cord made from deer sinew. He hoped it would bring him luck.

He walked toward the Place Where the Sun Goes at Night with the rising sun at his back. He had no plan, or, rather, his plan was to go where the Vision led him. He believed that as long as he heard the wolves calling, he was going where he was supposed to go. Their call was constant now but had faded to a low murmur in the back of his mind.

The message hadn't changed, though. The wolves were saying, "Come, Come."

He knew that the wolves wouldn't be close. He would have to go past where the scouts and hunters had already searched. He was anxious to get to this new land, so he began to run.

The People were great runners. One of the ways they hunted was to run their prey to exhaustion. Deer and bison were much faster than The People, but The People could run at the same speed all day. If they could stay close enough to the deer to keep them running, they would tire and then The People could close in and kill what they needed.

Wolf Finder was almost as good a runner as some of the hunters who were the best runners of all The People.

At first, when he began to run, he felt clumsy and didn't know why. Then he realized that it was the boots. He usually either went barefoot or with just a piece of hide tied around his foot. These new boots were heavy. He thought about taking them off, but the ground was still covered in snow. He would just have to get used to them.

By the time the sun was almost down to the Place Where the Sun Goes at Night he had come to a hill that he recognized. It was rocky with a single dead pine tree on top. This hill marked the farthest he had ever been away from home. He knew that the top would be free of snow and there were rocks where he could shelter. He also knew that there were marmots in the rocks, and a nice, big marmot would be perfect for dinner. He decided to spend the night there.

That evening as he lay on his robe and looked up at the stars he realized that this was the first night he had ever been completely alone. He missed his home. He missed The People. He missed Father and Mother. Looking at the vast sweep of sky above him he realized what a small, lonely little boy he was. He was far too small and weak for the great Quest he had been given.

But when he closed his eyes, the call of the wolves became louder, and he thought, *I am not alone. The wolves are with me. The wolves will help me.*

At the foot of Clay's bed, Gunny twitched and moaned, his sleep disturbed by something that was making him afraid.

CHAPTER TEN

Big Cat

THE WINTER HAD BEEN GOOD FOR RUNT'S PACK. It had been cold, and the snow was deep. The deer and other prey animals were having a hard time getting enough food, and that made them easier to hunt. It also seemed that the deer were not used to being hunted by wolves. They didn't stay close together in a tight group but tended to wander around in ones and twos so that the wolves had no problem separating out the weakest animal.

The more they hunted together, the better hunters they became. It was a rare night when they went to sleep without a full belly.

Runt was no longer a runt. With plenty of good food, he was now a fully-grown, adult male wolf. He was just a little smaller than Clown, and Sweetbreath was a little smaller than him.

They were a close-knit pack, but Runt and Sweetbreath were spending more and more time together. The pack had two dens. One for Runt and Sweetbreath and one for Clown. As the lowest ranking wolf in his former pack, Clown was used to being by himself, but Runt knew that he had a longing for a mate of his own.

For that is what Runt and Sweetbreath had become, a mated pair. In their small pack, they were the Alpha male and female. They treated

Clown like a brother, and they shared both food and the dangers of the hunt, but they were a pair, and Clown was alone.

With the passing of mid-winter, the wolves were traveling farther and farther each day to find the deer. The deer were moving toward the place where the sun comes up, and soon the pack had to follow. They moved their dens and then had to move again.

On the night of the first full moon after mid-winter, the pack was living in two dens on a hill in a small clearing. For Runt and Clown, it felt good not to be completely hemmed in by trees for a little while. Sweetbreath wasn't so happy.

As the moon rose to its full height, the three felt the primal urge to sing. Sitting on the top of their hill they lifted their muzzles to the sky and began to howl.

Wolves have many different howls. The one they did on this night was a sweet song of pure joy at being alive. When they had finished, they sat still and simply enjoyed the beauty of the night.

And then they heard another wolf howling back to them! This howl was weak, and it cracked from time to time. It was not a happy song. It was a call for help.

The three wolves howled a different song, *We hear you! We're coming!* They ran down the hill and into the forest.

The other wolf continued to howl. Just a couple of notes at a time with long pauses as if it couldn't catch its breath.

The pack was quiet now. They were cautious. Another pack might be luring them to a trap. It didn't make sense, but they wouldn't rush in until they knew what was really happening.

Soon, they were close enough to begin to get the wolf's scent. They moved even slower, constantly sniffing for any sign of danger. They could only smell one wolf even when they went around in a wide circle. They could smell blood. When they were sure the wolf was alone they moved in carefully.

What they found was a young female cowering under some tree branches. As they came close, she tucked her tail and lowered her head and whimpered. Runt and Clown stood back, and Sweetbreath walked up to the new wolf and sniffed her carefully. She then went back to Runt and Clown and indicated with her head that they should all lie down.

After a few minutes, the new wolf cautiously stood and approached them. Carefully and slowly she began to sniff each wolf. When she had finished, her head was up, and her tail was starting to wag. These wolves were not going to hurt her. But would they accept her into their pack?

If they didn't, she would die.

Runt looked at Sweetbreath and Clown and saw that they were thinking the same thing he was. He and Sweetbreath stood and began to walk slowly back toward the den. Clown walked over to the young female and with a gentle nudge told her to follow.

Even with Runt, Sweetbreath, and Clown breaking trail ahead of her, the new wolf was having trouble making her way through the snow. She was on her last legs. There was nothing Runt could do for her until they got back to the den, so he just walked slowly and paused from time to time to let her rest. When they stopped, Clown would stand on one side of her and Sweetbreath on the other to support her and share some of their warmth. When they got close to the den, Clown ran ahead to dig up some of the deer meat that they had stored from their last kill.

The new wolf had just enough strength to make it up the hill before she collapsed. Clown was there with a mouthful of meat that he had chewed so that it would be warm and easy to eat. It was something he used to do for the puppies.

When he put the food down in front of her, the young wolf just sniffed and didn't move. Then her tongue came out and licked at the fresh meat. Next, she took a nibble. Then she gobbled it down.

She was too tired to stand, but she could eat. Runt thought that was a good sign.

After several helpings of food, she was able to stand, and Runt got his first good look at her in the light of the moon. She was about his age, but she was small and very thin. He saw that the fur along her right side was matted with blood. Sweetbreath walked up to her and began to lick at a wound that looked like it had come from the claws of some large animal. The cut didn't look very deep, but for a young wolf on her own, even a minor injury could be enough to make hunting difficult. It was clear she hadn't been eating well. She was trembling, and Runt didn't know if she was afraid, or just cold.

While Sweetbreath tended to her wound, Runt walked around to her front. She turned to look at him, and when the moon shone directly on her face Runt took a step back and let out a little bark of surprise.

Runt didn't know exactly why — it was some combination of shape and black, white, and grey colors — but this young female had the most beautiful face he'd ever seen.

When she had eaten some more, it was time for sleep. The new wolf sniffed at Runt's den and then Clown's den, and without hesitation crawled into Clown's den. Clown looked at Runt with an almost comical expression of confusion. Runt gave Clown a wolf shrug and joined Sweetbreath in his den. In a minute he heard Clown crawling into his den with the new wolf.

There were now four wolves in Runt's pack.

For the next moon-change, the primary job of Runt's pack was trying to get Beauty healthy and strong. At first, she was too weak to leave the den hill on her own. Clown usually stayed with her while Runt and Sweetbreath hunted rabbits nearby. They couldn't hunt deer with just two wolves, there was too much chance of a wolf getting hurt. Fortunately, since they had been hunting deer almost exclusively, there were plenty of rabbits around, and they continued to eat well.

Beauty was wary of Runt and Sweetbreath. Whenever one of them would approach her, she would tuck her tail and lower her head as if she expected them to attack her. She was even submissive with Clown, who was as mild-mannered as it was possible for a wolf to be.

Runt thought that she must have had a problem with an Alpha wolf in her last pack the way he'd had with Scar. She may have been forced out of her pack and not have been as lucky as he was to have another wolf like Clown to help her. A young female wolf on her own would have a tough time. She was lucky just to be alive.

When her strength began to return, and her wounded side was almost healed, Beauty started going on hunts with the rest of the pack. She was not as big and strong as the others, but she was fast and nimble, which made her the best rabbit hunter. When she went on her first deer hunt, Sweetbreath took her to help drive the deer toward Runt and Clown. Again, Beauty's speed and quickness was an asset. She was almost as fast as a deer, and she could turn more quickly to cut them off before they could get away.

Soon, the pack was back to eating deer almost every day.

A few days after the next full moon Runt realized that the deer were moving again and the pack would have to follow. He didn't like leaving their dens on the hill, but he had no choice. The next morning he led the wolves down off their hill and into the forest heading again toward the place where the sun comes up.

Runt was feeling good. He enjoyed being the pack leader. Four wolves were not a large pack, but they were all strong and healthy, and they worked well together. The only rival predators they had seen were a couple of bears who seemed content to leave the wolves alone as long as the wolves left them alone. Runt was happy to do that.

Runt was hoping to find another hill like the one they had just left, but the best he could do was a low outcropping of rocks. There were some small caves there which meant that they wouldn't have to dig a den, but the clearing was small and didn't feel as comfortable.

Sweetbreath and Beauty seemed to think that the new den area was just fine and set about to select their caves. The two females selected caves that were close to each other. Runt watched Clown cautiously approach Beauty's cave. Runt was sure that Clown expected to hear a growl telling him to go find his own cave. When Beauty instead made a soft *woof* inviting Clown to join her, the look of happiness on Clown's face was so funny that Runt gave out a high-pitched bark, which is as close as a wolf can come to laughing.

For the first few days, it looked as though the pack had found a good home. There were plenty of prey animals nearby, and their den area was snug and comfortable. On the next hunt, however, everything changed.

Runt was loping along with the scent of deer in his nostrils when he crossed a track that made him almost skid to a stop. It was big, much bigger than a wolf track and only a little smaller than a bear track. He took a sniff and didn't recognize the scent, but he instinctively knew it was something dangerous.

Sweetbreath checked the new track next. It was the track that Mother had warned her about when they first left their pack. Beauty took one sniff and turned and ran. Clown ran after Beauty.

When Runt and Sweetbreath found them, Beauty was curled up in the snow and shaking. Clown was licking her muzzle and trying to comfort her. Runt didn't understand, but then he had a thought. He went to Beauty and began to sniff her side where she'd been wounded. He hadn't paid much attention to Beauty's injury; Clown and Sweetbreath had taken care of her. Now he sniffed long and hard, parting her fur with his nose to get close to the skin. It was there, just as he'd thought. It was very faint, but it was the same scent as on the new tracks they had found.

Runt didn't know what this new animal was, but he knew it was a predator, and it was a danger to the pack. He had to do something about this, but first, he had to find out exactly what kind of threat he was facing. Clown and Beauty were frightened, but they would have to get over it. This was a problem for the whole pack, and they would have to face it together.

Runt turned to head back to where he had found the track. Sweetbreath followed, and Clown began to follow too, but when he saw that Beauty was still lying in the snow, he stopped.

Runt turned and trotted calmly back to Beauty. He nudged her to try to get her to move, but she just lay there. Runt stood and fluffed his fur out to make himself look as big as possible and let out a low warning growl.

When Beauty still didn't move, he attacked.

It looked vicious, and it was meant to. Runt was snarling and growling, and his huge teeth were snapping at Beauty's fur. Runt was careful not to actually hurt her, but he had to make her follow the pack. If she couldn't or wouldn't, then he would do whatever he had to do. There was no room in his pack for a wolf who would not help her packmates.

When Runt stepped back, Beauty stood. Runt watched carefully as she looked at Clown and Sweetbreath. In their eyes, she saw sadness but no pity. She understood that whatever happened the other wolves would support Runt. It was The Law of the Pack.

Beauty turned and looked at Runt. He could see the mix of emotions playing in her face and eyes. Her body was taut, and she trembled. Then she made her decision, and Runt could see her body relax and her eyes clear. She lay down and rolled over exposing her belly to Runt. Runt stood over her and let his fur lay back. He leaned down and gently licked her muzzle, then turned and went to find this new threat to the pack.

Three determined wolves followed him.

The track was easy to follow. This new predator was making no effort to hide. In fact, Runt thought that he was trying to let all the other animals in the forest know he was there. He had spray marked on several trees and bushes which is how Runt knew it was a male. The more Runt learned about this animal, the more worried he became.

When they had followed his track for a while Runt began to get the scent of deer, and then the smell of blood. The track changed direction suddenly, and the distance between each paw print more than doubled. Runt began to see deer tracks. The animal was chasing deer. Not just one deer as the wolves would do, but a whole herd. The smell of blood became stronger.

The track went into a small clearing, and when Runt saw what was there, he stopped dead. In front of him were the bodies of three deer who hadn't just been killed, they'd been torn apart. Runt had been on hunts with his old pack where the wolves had killed more than one deer. Some wolves just seemed to enjoy killing, but he had never seen anything like this.

The other wolves gathered in close to Runt. They stood there for a long time just looking. Then Runt shook his head to clear his mind.

This was a dangerous place. They didn't know where this new predator might be. They had to find him and decide how they would deal with him.

Runt began to follow the tracks past the dead deer. He saw that the predator had eaten. Large pieces of meat were missing from each deer, but he had left much behind. Did that mean he was planning to come back?

The wolves were moving slowly and carefully now with their noses working as hard as they could. The wind was behind them which meant that the predator would smell them before they could smell him. That made Runt very nervous.

Runt was trotting across a small clearing when the track suddenly stopped. There was a clear track of the big animal walking, then a place where the snow was disturbed in an odd way, then ... nothing.

Just then the wind shifted, and Runt got the scent of the predator. The scent was strong, the animal was close, but where?

Beauty gave a very soft bark. When Runt turned to look at her, he saw that she was looking up at the trees just in front of them. Runt followed her eyes, and there he was. In a tree!

Runt knew that there were little cats that could climb, but this thing was big, three times or more the size of a big wolf. It was almost golden in color with sleek fur. It sat in the tree calmly licking the blood off its paws. Runt didn't notice much else because all his attention was on the animal's massive jaws and teeth. It was easy to see how he had torn those deer apart so completely.

The animal seemed calm and unconcerned about the four wolves looking at him, but what would he do next?

Runt's question was answered in an instant when Big Cat, moving faster than any animal he had ever seen, leaped out of the tree and landed a few feet in front of him.

Runt was so startled by what Big Cat had done that he was unable to move for a couple of critical seconds. Sweetbreath and Clown were just as shocked as Runt and couldn't help.

The only one who could react was Beauty. It wasn't the first time she'd seen this killer, and she was terrified. Her first instinct was to run, but she remembered that Runt and the other wolves had saved her life. She couldn't let this horrible creature kill them.

Big Cat tensed to pounce, but Beauty reacted first. Snarling and growling she sprang at his side and got a quick bite in before nimbly jumping away.

The big cat spun around after Beauty, but Runt was over his shock, and he jumped in to get a bite on the cat's hip. Clown and Sweetbreath joined the fight with quick nips that didn't do much more than briefly distract Big Cat.

The fight was now a free-for-all. None of the wolves had been hurt, but Big Cat's wounds weren't serious, and he was quicker and stronger. Runt saw Beauty run past Big Cat and into the trees. At first, Runt thought she was running away, but then he realized she was trying to distract the cat from the rest of them. As Big Cat turned to go after Beauty, Runt ran at his backside and got a bite of his tail as he went past.

The other two wolves saw what Runt and Beauty were doing, and they did the same. It was working, Big Cat was turning in one direction then the other, and he couldn't focus on any one wolf. The problem was that the wolves were being separated with each one going in a different direction.

After just a few seconds Big Cat tired. He'd just eaten, and he was sluggish. The wolves saw their chance and ran as fast as they could to get away.

They ran in four different directions and quickly lost track of each other.

CHAPTER ELEVEN

Iwo Jima and the Buffalo Wheel

WHEN CLAY AWOKE, HE WAS DISORIENTED AND CONFUSED. It seemed that one minute he had been Wolf Finder setting out on a quest into the forest, and the next minute he was in a comfortable bed with a sea breeze blowing in the window.

Gunny got up from where he'd been sleeping and came over. He put his paws up on the bed and looked at Clay.

"What's happening, Gunny? Why did I have that dream? But it wasn't a dream, it was like I was remembering something from a long time ago. This is weird."

Clay sat for a long time thinking.

Who can I talk to about this? If I tell Mom or Dad, they'll just think I was dreaming about all the stuff I've been talking about with Coop. Coop'll think the same thing. But it wasn't a dream. It was like I was really there. But how can that be? Who can I talk to?

After a few more minutes of thought, Clay made a decision and went to find his sister.

"… and then I woke up and I was in my bed and not in the forest.

"That's the story. What do you guys think? Am I crazy?"

"I liked your story very much," Iben said.

"I also liked your story, and I do not think that you are crazy," Maia said.

"Of course you're crazy. You've always been crazy, but that doesn't mean your dream wasn't real."

"Thanks, Mara. I think.

"Do you guys believe me?"

All three girls nodded.

"OK, so what do I do?"

"That's easy," Mara said, "Go talk to Grandpa Sam."

"Grandpa Sam?"

"Sure. You remember the time Grandpa Sam was talking to Dad, and they didn't know we were listening, and he was tellin' about when he and Gunny went to Iwo Jima to find those Marines who died in World War II."

"Yeah, that's right, and Grandpa Sam was talking about the strange dreams they had that seemed like they saw things that really happened in the battle, and those dreams helped them find the guys they were lookin' for."

"Yeah, and those dreams sound a lot like the dream you had."

"You think Grandpa might believe me about my dream?"

"If he won't, nobody will."

"OK, I'll go talk to him."

"Uh-uh, we'll go talk to him. You got us into this, you're not gonna get rid of us now. Right, girls?"

Maia and Iben nodded with big smiles.

"All right, all right, you're in. But before we talk to Grandpa, I've gotta try to tell you all the stuff I learned from Coop, so you'll know what I'm talkin' about."

"We're all ears," Mara said.

Clay never had a chance to talk with Coop that morning. When Coop wasn't busy getting ready to leave, the adults were taking all his time. Clay was a little disappointed, but a little relieved, too. He wasn't sure what he could say after last night's dream.

The adults were taking Coop out for brunch and then to the Jacksonville airport. As they were getting ready to leave, Coop pulled Clay aside

"I'm sorry we didn't get a chance to finish our discussion. I enjoyed talking to you and trying to answer your questions."

"Yeah, I enjoyed it too, and I learned a lot. There's still a lot I don't understand, though."

"I know. Look, here's my e-mail address. You send me your questions, and I'll try to answer them, or I'll send you a link to something you can read to learn for yourself. Does that sound fair?"

"Sure! Thanks for spending so much time with a dumb kid."

"You may be a kid, but you're not dumb. Keep asking those hard questions, and you'll be fine."

When it was time, the two sets of parents went with Coop, and Grandpa Sam and Grandma Rebecca stayed to watch the kids.

That made things a lot easier for Clay and the girls.

◆ ◆ ◆

Grandpa and Grandma were on the porch reading when Clay and the girls walked up. Grandpa looked at Clay and knew something was going on.

"Hey, Clay. What's up?"

"Grandpa, Iben and Maia and Mara and I'd like to talk with you for a little while."

"OK, sure."

"Uh, could we talk to you alone?"

Sam looked at Clay with a slight frown, "Kids, your Grandma and I have been together for a long, long time. There's nothing you can tell me that she shouldn't hear."

"OK, but this is kinda strange. I don't want you guys to get upset with us, and, if you do, it's my fault."

"OK, now you've got my attention," Grandma Rebecca said, "What is it?"

"Well, it's kinda weird. It's about the dreams you had on Iwo Jima when you and Gunny were there."

"How do you know about that?"

"We listened to you and Dad talkin' one night," Mara said.

"That'll teach me to keep my big mouth shut. OK, what do you want to know?"

"I think I've had dreams the last couple of nights that're like the dreams you had."

"You mean you dreamt about the battle of Iwo Jima?"

"No, no, I mean I had a dream that was like I was remembering something, and I was seeing things through another kid's eyes, just like you told Dad you did."

"OK, what did you dream about?"

"You know what I've been talkin' about with Coop, right?"

"Yeah, it was very interesting listening to you two."

"Last night I dreamed that I was the Oldest Boy of The People and we couldn't find the wolves, and the wolves were calling to me, and …."

"Whoa, whoa, slow down. Let's go back to the beginning and tell me the whole story."

"OK, this all happened a long, long time ago …"

"So, let me make sure I understand this, Clay. Tell me again exactly how it felt while you were having this dream."

"OK, …it felt like I was actually Oldest Boy. I saw things through his eyes, I heard things through his ears, I even smelled what he was smelling. Is that anything like your dreams, Grandpa?"

Sam was quiet for a long moment and then looked at Rebecca who nodded.

"It's a lot like the dreams I had on Iwo Jima. I dreamed I was a young Marine named Robby Durance, who was one of the missing men we were searching for. I dreamed that I was Robby during the battle for Iwo Jima, and it was pretty scary, I'll tell ya. Was your dream scary?"

"No, it was actually kinda … interesting? Fun? I wasn't scared. Do you believe me, Grandpa?"

"I don't think you're making this up, and your dream sounds too much like mine to be a coincidence, so, yeah, I believe you."

"Thanks, Grandpa."

"But now the question is, why? Why did you have this dream? I can understand my dream — well, as much as I can understand any of this stuff. In my dream, the ghost of Robby Durance was trying to help us find his remains and the remains of the Marines who died with him. But why would you dream about being a boy fifteen thousand years ago?"

"I don't know, but I have a feeling it has something to do with Gunny."

"Gunny? Why?"

"You know he's been sleeping in my room the last few nights, right?"

"Yeah, I thought that was a little strange."

"Well, I only have these dreams when Gunny is around, and he keeps looking at me funny."

"What do you mean?"

"He looks at me like, … I dunno, like he's trying to tell me something."

"Sam, I just had a thought," Rebecca said,

"What?"

"What's the one thing that's in common with your dreams, Clay's dreams, and all the other strange things that happened on Iwo Jima and up at the Buffalo Wheel?"

"I don't know, I haven't thought — wait a minute … Gunny! Gunny was there when me and the others were having those dreams, and he's the one that Japanese demon was trying to kill, and he and the other three dogs turned into wolves at the Buffalo Wheel. Gunny is the only one who was there for everything."

"Wait … stop, …. Whatta you mean …?" the four kids asked at once, "What demon? What wolves?"

"Sorry guys," Sam said, "There were a lot of strange things that happened on Iwo and up at the Buffalo Wheel that we haven't told you about. Grandma and I are gonna have to talk to your parents before we talk about this 'cause some of it's kinda scary.

"But you're right, Rebecca, Gunny is the only one who's been there when all of these things happened. Somehow, this is all about Gunny."

As if he'd been called, Gunny walked into the room, sat in front of Sam, barked twice, and looked at everyone with a broad, open-mouth grin on his face.

"It's like he's saying, 'About time you figured this out,'" Rebecca said.

Turning to Iben, Rebecca asked, "Sweetheart, you're the youngest one here. Is this scary for you?"

Iben looked up at the ceiling and then back at Rebecca, "A little, maybe, but also very interesting."

"What about the rest of you?" Sam asked, "Is any of this scaring you?"

"Uh-uh," Mara and Maia said together.

"I think it's cool!" Clay said.

"Yeah, Clay, that figures," Rebecca said with a smile.

"OK," Sam said, "Here's what I'd like to do. Let's forget all this stuff for a while. We need to get out on the beach, anyway.

"Clay, you and Grandma and I will talk to your parents and Aunt Maddie and Uncle Knut. You tell them about your dream. Then, if it's OK with them, we'll have a little family meeting tonight, and Grandma and I will tell everyone about all the strange things that happened on those two searches. Then maybe we can all figure out what's going on with Clay's dreams.

"That OK with you, Bec?"

"Yeah, that sounds like a good idea," Rebecca replied, "You guys OK with that?"

When everyone had nodded agreement, Rebecca said, "Good. Let's go get our beach clothes on and have some fun for a while, and we'll worry about this other stuff later."

After the four kids had run out of the room, Sam and Rebecca just looked at each other for a minute and then looked at Gunny who was still sitting there, smiling.

"I keep thinking we've left all the weird stuff behind us, but it keeps following us around," Sam said, "Now I guess we know why. Our dog seems to be a link into … what? The spirit world? Some other dimension?"

"I don't know," Rebecca said, "But it's not Gunny's fault. You're a good dog, aren't you Gunny?"

Gunny barked twice in agreement.

That afternoon Clay, Sam, and Rebecca sat down with both sets of parents and had a long talk. They agreed to a family meeting after dinner.

Later, after a quiet dinner, the family gathered in the living room. Clay's Aunt Maddie was the first to speak, and she talked directly to the four kids.

"We're here to talk because Clay has been having some strange dreams, and we want to help him understand what they mean. We've all just learned about some of the peculiar things that happened with Grandpa and Gunny on their last two searches, and we need to talk about that, too. Some of this might be a little scary. We want all you kids to promise that if you start feeling scared or worried, you'll let us know right away so we can help. Does everyone agree?

All four kids responded with some version of, "Yes, Ma'am."

"OK, Dad," Maddie said, "You're up."

"Thanks, Mad, good job.

"Before I start, do any of you have any questions about what we've talked about so far?"

"Yes, Grandpa, I do."

"What, Maia?"

"Do you believe in ghosts?"

"Maia, in America that's what we call, 'cutting to the chase.' That means getting right to the heart of an issue.

"I've thought about this a lot over the last two years, and the best answer I can give you is that I don't not-believe. Does that make sense to you?"

Maia thought for a moment, "Does that mean that you think there might be ghosts, but you are not sure?"

"That's an excellent way to put it. I'm glad Maia asked that question because I'm not here to try to tell you what you should or shouldn't believe about the strange things that happened on Iwo Jima and up at the Buffalo Wheel. I'll try to tell you as accurately as I can what I saw, and Grandma will talk about what she saw. Ask all the questions you want, and we'll try to answer. When we're done, each of you will have to decide what you think really happened.

"OK?"

"Yes, Grandpa," the four kids said together.

"OK, here we go. I'll start with the search on Iwo Jima. I think you all know the basics. I was contacted by someone from a group called Team Liberty. He told me that there were still some Marines whose remains were never recovered after the battle. He wanted me and Gunny to go to Iwo Jima to help his team look for the bodies of five young men. We became part of a search team with an explosive detection dog named Luke, a forensic anthropologist, a historian, and a team leader.

"Shortly after we got to the island I started having very realistic dreams about the battle. In those dreams, I was a young Marine in combat for the first time. Just like Clay's dream, I saw what was happening through his eyes, and heard through his ears. I could feel his fear, and it was pretty darn scary, I can tell you.

"Now, Iwo Jima is a pretty scary place. It's a volcanic island. Iwo Jima means, 'Sulfur Island,' and it smells like you might imagine hell would smell. Twenty-six thousand Americans and Japanese were killed there in thirty-six days of fighting. I figured I was just having strange dreams because of where I was and what I knew about the battle.

"Later, I found out that I wasn't the only one having strange dreams. Both Luke's handler and our team leader were having the same dreams. These two were combat veterans; a former Marine who lost a leg in Afghanistan, and an Army Ranger. The other members of the team, our historian, our forensic anthropologist, and another forensic anthropologist from Japan, were civilians and had never been in combat. They never had the dreams, but they all saw what they thought was the ghost of a man dressed as a Marine from 1945."

"Why did they think it was a ghost?" Mara asked.

"Good question. This image or apparition, or whatever you want to call it seemed to be able to appear and disappear and walk through a chain link fence like it wasn't there. It never spoke, and whenever it appeared, whoever saw it would feel like they'd just stepped into a cold bath."

"Sounds like a ghost to me," Clay said.

"Yep, that's what we thought. Does that answer your question, Mara?"

"Yeah, thanks."

"Eventually, we got together and compared stories and figured that those of us who were combat veterans were all dreaming of being the same young Marine, Robby Durance, and we guessed that it was also his ghost that was appearing to the others. We also guessed that Gunny and Luke were dreaming about him."

"Why did you think that, Dad?" Mike asked.

"There were several things, but the main one was that the first find that Gunny had was a piece of bone. He should have had to be within a few feet of that seventy-year-old bone to get its scent, but he got it from about sixty yards away. When we started comparing notes on all the strange things we'd seen, it seemed to make sense that he'd gotten some sort of supernatural help.

"Then we found out that there was another ghost, or, more accurately, a demon."

"How did you figure that out?" Knut asked.

"We actually heard it yelling at Gunny in Japanese. Our Japanese forensic anthropologist said that what we heard was a Japanese demon trying to lure Gunny to where he would step on an old mine and be killed. Fortunately, Luke saved Gunny at the last second.

"Finally, when we went to the funeral at Arlington Cemetery for the five Marines we found, we all saw their ghosts as we were leaving the grave site."

"How do you know they were ghosts?" Maddie asked.

"Well, Gunny and Luke noticed them first, I think they smelled them, and then these five young men dressed in old Marine uniforms appeared under a tree. Gunny and Luke ran to them like they were old friends. Then one of them, Robby Durance, the one we dreamed about, walked toward us and spoke. He thanked us for finding them and bringing them home, and he said that we would see him again someday and understand what this was all about."

"Dad, that is beyond a doubt the strangest thing I've ever heard you say," Maddie said.

"That's what I saw too," Rebecca said, "I agree it was strange, but we all saw it."

"To summarize," Sam continued, "Six intelligent, well-educated people all had various experiences during a search on Iwo Jima and later at Arlington National Cemetery that we could only believe were some sort of paranormal phenomena."

"How did you explain that?" Maddie asked.

"We couldn't, but we rationalized it by remembering all the young men who had died on that island. We thought that if there were ghosts anywhere in the world, then they would be there on Iwo Jima. Then we agreed that we wouldn't talk about this to anyone, so that's why I haven't told any of you, except Rebecca and Mike, about this before.

"Any questions?"

"Yes, Grandpa, what does, 'paranor …,' that word you used, mean?"

"Sorry, Maia. It means something that is outside of what's normal, something that can't be explained by things we understand."

"Like a ghost?"

"Yes, like a ghost."

After a long silence, Sam continued, "OK, now let's talk about the Buffalo Wheel. I'll give you the background, but I'll let Bec tell you about the really strange things that happened there since she had a much better view of them than I did.

"I went over this once when we talked with Coop, but all the ladies were at the aquarium so I'll just summarize for them.

"We went to the Bighorn Mountains of Wyoming to a place the native tribes call the Buffalo Wheel to look for a possible burial site. Sees Wolf, an Arapaho medicine man, thought that someone might have been buried there improperly and that this person's spirit might be interfering with their sacred ceremonies."

"He thought it was Butch Cassidy," Clay said.

"That's right, and it may have been," Sam said, "and the problem is that Jake Cooley, a meth dealer who lived near the Arapaho Reservation, got the idea that what was buried there was some loot from one of Butch's train robberies. He's the one that caused all the trouble.

"We were there with Luke, the explosive detection dog from our search on Iwo Jima and his handler, plus a new search dog, named Iwo."

"Cool name," Clay said.

"Yes," Rebecca replied, "A Golden Retriever from the same breeder where we got Gunny. He was a present from your Grandfather to the woman who was the forensic anthropologist on the Iwo Jima search. Pretty darn expensive present."

"Yes, Dear. May I continue?"

Rebecca nodded with a smile.

"We also had Sees Wolf and his nephew Joseph Golden Eagle and some Arapaho cowboys to help with the horses and equipment.

"Why horses?" Knut asked

"We were on a National Historic Landmark. Motorized vehicles weren't allowed at the Wheel."

"OK, so that was your whole team?"

"Well, there was *hooxei*."

"Who, or what is *hooxei*?" Hannah asked.

"*Hooxei* is Sees Wolf's spirit wolf. Sees Wolf got his name because his spirit brother is a wolf," Rebecca replied, "If you were an Arapaho, all of this would seem perfectly normal to you."

"OK," Hannah replied, "I suppose *hooxei* has a role in what happens next?"

"Oh, yeah, a big role," Rebecca replied, "He saved my life."

"I thought the dogs saved your life," Hannah said.

"That's the story we told the authorities afterward during the investigation. The truth is quite a bit stranger. Let Bec finish," Sam said.

"OK, I can't wait."

"Me neither!" Clay said.

"OK, let me set the scene, and then Rebecca can finish.

"The dogs found the buried remains about a half mile from the Wheel. Actually, the dogs had a little help from *hooxei*."

"How do you know the dogs had help from the spirit wolf?" Knut asked.

"Because we heard him howl."

Everyone stared at Sam silently.

"You think that's strange? We're just getting' started."

"OK, so we found the remains, and headed back to where the cars were parked, and we were in the middle of a blizzard. It was June, but up at ninety-six hundred feet in the Bighorns it can snow anytime.

"Waiting for us when we got to the cars was Jake Cooley. Cooley was big and mean, and he had a couple of guns. Turns out that he was probably crazy from the effects of life-long alcoholism.

"Anyway, he took Rebecca as a hostage and had one of the cowboys tie us up. He was gonna ride off with Rebecca on his ATV, but the cowboy stole his keys and threw them off into the snow. He almost got shot for that. Cooley ended up dragging Bec off into the woods.

"As soon as we got untied, I sent Gunny off to search for Rebecca. I'll let her pick up the story from there."

"It was snowing so hard you couldn't see more than a few feet. The first thing that happened after Cooley grabbed me was we fell down a long, snow-covered slope and I got pretty banged up," Rebecca began, "I knew Gunny would be able to find me, but I was worried about what Cooley might do when he did.

"He dragged me along with him for a ways and finally stopped in a little clearing in the woods. Sure enough, a few minutes later, here comes Gunny."

Gunny looked over at Rebecca.

"Yes, you were a very good dog that day."

Gunny smiled.

"Cooley took a shot at Gunny, and, well, you can see the scar on his hip. Gunny didn't stop, though. He went back and found Sam, just like he's trained to do, and then turned around to lead him back to me.

"Then things started getting really weird.

"I was standing there in the snow. Cooley had his big, beefy arm around me and was holding his pistol to my head, just waiting for Sam and the others to show up. Then, from out of the snow-covered forest came the scariest sound I've ever heard — the sound of a pack of wolves on the hunt.

"A few seconds later, I saw four huge wolves charge out of the woods running right toward us. Cooley was so frightened he let go of me and dropped his gun. The lead wolf leaped up and got Cooley's arm in his jaws, and, well, he just about took his arm off."

"Mom! Are you kidding me?" Mike asked.

"Nope. I will never forget the scream that Cooley made. He dropped like a sack of potatoes and tried to curl up into a little ball.

"I was lying in the snow a few feet away, and these four wolves were gathered around Cooley, and I knew that they were going to tear him apart. Then, one of the wolves looked at me. When I saw his eyes, I recognized him immediately."

"You recognized a wolf?" Maddie asked.

"Yep. It was Gunny."

"Gunny was a wolf?"

"Yep, and then I realized that two of the other wolves were Luke and Iwo. Then the lead wolf looked at me. He was the most frightening, and most beautiful, animal I've ever seen.

"They were about to tear Cooley apart, and he probably deserved it, but I said, 'Don't!' and they stopped.

"Then two men riding horses bare-backed, with bare chests, wearing war paint and eagle feathers galloped into the clearing. They were both carrying rifles, and I recognized them too. It was Sees Wolf and Golden Eagle somehow transformed into ancient Arapaho warriors.

"Sees Wolf called to the lead wolf, who was, of course, *hooxei* in the flesh, and said something to him in Arapaho. *Hooxei* looked back at Cooley like he was disappointed that he wasn't gonna get to chew on him some more and then just trotted off into the woods.

"When I turned to look back at Gunny, he and the others had turned back into dogs. Gunny was badly hurt, and I was afraid he was gonna die, but Luke's handler and our forensic anthropologist went to work on him and, well, here he is.

"They tried to save Cooley, too, but he was hurt too badly. He died in the hospital in Casper a couple of days later from a combination of his injuries and the effects of alcoholism."

"Is that it?" Mike asked.

"Yep, that's our story, and we're stickin' to it," Sam said, "Any questions?"

"Only a few hundred," Mike said, "This is a lot of stuff to try to understand."

"Yeah," Sam said, "It took us a while to take it in, and we had the advantage of being able to talk to the others who were there. All I can say is that there were six or seven of us who all saw the same things. None of us saw everything, but we all saw enough that we agree on the basic stories."

"May I ask a question?"

"Of course, Knut."

"The Arapahoe medicine man you mentioned, Sees Wolf?"

"Yes."

"Is that Doctor Edward Sees Wolf?"

"His first name, or as he says his, 'white name,' is Edward but I don't think he ever said he was a Doctor. I know he went to the University of Wyoming on a rodeo scholarship, but he never talked much about his education beyond that."

"I'm sure he's the same person. I think you know that my field of study is cultural anthropology, and I did my doctoral and post-doctoral work on the traditions and beliefs concerning witch doctors in the native tribes of Tanzania."

"Yes, of course."

"Doctor Sees Wolf is well respected in my specialty area because he is both a researcher and an actual medicine man. I've spoken to him several times at different conferences."

"I had no idea he was a cultural anthropologist," Sam said, "Although, now that I think about it, it makes sense. He looked like an Arapaho cowboy, but he's one of the smartest people I've ever met. What do you think of him?"

Knut furrowed his brows in thought for a minute, then said, "I am a very down-to-earth sort of person. I'm not the type to read fantasy or sci-fi stories. I like to deal in facts. However, I have seen things while I lived among the tribespeople in Tanzania for which I have no logical explanation. So, when I hear a well-educated, intelligent man like Doctor Sees Wolf talk about the reality of some of the things in the Arapaho religion, like spirit wolves, for example, I pay attention.

"Would you mind if I contact Doctor Sees Wolf to discuss what you've just told us?"

"My only concern is that we promised him and the others not to talk about this stuff. What do you think, Bec?"

"Honestly?" Rebecca said, "I think Sees Wolf would love to tell Knut about what it felt like to turn into an ancient Arapaho warrior."

Sam chuckled, "Yeah, I think you're right. OK, Knut, I'll get you his e-mail and phone number. Let us know what you find out."

"Thank you. If he's in Wyoming, he's two hours behind us. I may try to call him tonight."

"OK, great."

"I'm almost afraid to ask, but, 'Any other questions?'"

Sam looked at each member of the family. They all seemed lost in thought.

"All right then, I think the best thing for all of you to do is to just let this sit for a while and see what you think later. In the meantime, Bec and I will be happy to talk or answer any questions you think of.

"Remember though, the reason we told you all about this is so we could help Clay figure out what his dream was about. I think we should focus on that now."

"I don't know about anyone else," Mike said, "But I'd like to take a long walk on the beach with Clay before we do anything else."

"Good idea," Rebecca said, "Do we want to meet back here in an hour?"

After a general murmur of agreement, the meeting adjourned.

It was almost completely dark by the time the family got back together. It was a lovely evening with a gentle breeze off the ocean, and they elected to sit outside on the screen porch.

When everyone had settled in, Mike was the first to speak, "Clay and I had a nice, long talk. He remembers his dream very well, and I don't think he's making anything up, and his memory of the dream does sound a lot like the dreams his Grandpa had on Iwo Jima. The question in my mind is, 'What do we do now?'"

"The first thing to remember," Sam said, "Is that there is one key difference between Clay's dream and mine. Clay's dream didn't have anything scary or evil in it. Right, Clay?"

"Yeah, Grandpa. It was mostly interesting. I never felt scared."

"Good. There's no reason to believe that anything bad is going to happen, but if that changes, Clay, if you start getting scared or worried, you need to let your Mom or Dad know right away."

"Right. I already promised Dad I would."

"Good. I suggest we just enjoy this nice evening and head off to bed and we'll see what happens tonight."

Everyone agreed, and, soon, the conversation turned to things that had nothing to do with ghosts or spirits.

That night, Gunny went to sleep immediately at the foot of Clay's bed and began to dream of Runt, and the pack.

Clay thought that he would lie awake for a long time thinking about all the things he had learned from Grandpa and Grandma. Instead, he listened to Gunny's snores for a few minutes and then fell into a dream.

CHAPTER TWELVE

The Wolves Howl

IT TOOK A LONG TIME FOR WOLF FINDER TO LEAVE HIS ROCKY HILL the next morning. He told himself that it was because he was tired, but he knew that the truth was that he was frightened of going into the unknown.

Then, he remembered what he'd said to himself the night before:

I am not alone. The wolves are with me. The wolves will help me.

He began to walk down the hill.

For the next two days, he went more slowly. He knew that the hunters and scouts had not gone far from home since the snows began and he thought that he might begin to see sign of wolves. He saw sign of many animals, but no wolves.

By the end of his third day on the Quest, he understood what First Scout had told him about the forest. Before him, all he could see were pine trees that grew so close together they looked like a green wall. Even with the sun high in the sky, he could see that it was dark there in the trees.

It should have been frightening, but he had put his fear behind him now. He had put his faith in the Vision. He would succeed or fail, he would live or die, but he would not let fear stop him. To prove to himself that he was not afraid, he didn't stop but walked straight into the thick woods.

The snow was deeper here where there was little sun or wind. The deeper snow would make walking harder, but it could be helpful, too, because the tracks of animals were easy to find.

He would have to learn many things about this forest. There would be new animals, and the animals he knew would behave differently, and he would have to learn how to hunt them. There would be new dangers, and he would have to be alert. In the back of his mind was always the picture of Big Cat that his father had shown him. No one knew if Big Cat lived in this part of the forest. He hoped he wouldn't find out.

After three more days, he was beginning to understand this forest better. It wasn't as thick everywhere as it had been when he had first seen it. There were places where it was like the forest near home, and most of the animals could be found in these places. There were many small animals, and he was able to keep himself well fed. He learned that he could build a snow cave under a downed tree and stay warm even when his fire had died down.

That night he went to sleep with the call of the wolves in his head. For the first time, he actually dreamt of wolves. He saw four of them running in the snow through the forest. He had never seen wolves run, but he knew that this was what they would look like.

His dream began to fade, and the call of the wolves became louder. But something was different. The call didn't sound the same. It wasn't just strange noises it seemed more like a …

A howl! Wolf Finder sat up so quickly he banged his head on a tree branch. *The wolves are howling! I can hear them with my ears!*

He sat mesmerized, listening to the deep, rich sounds of a beautiful song that went on and on. The sounds were faint, so the wolves weren't close, but they couldn't be far, either. It was hard to be sure, but it sounded like the howling was coming from the direction he had been traveling, and there was one more thing. He could hear four different voices. There were four wolves.

He had been right to trust the Vision. It had led him to the wolves.

It was almost dark, and Runt had been searching for his packmates since the fight with Big Cat. They were his wolves, and he was responsible for them. He was worried.

When the wolves ran, they used every trick they knew to disguise their track or hide their scent. Runt would find a track and follow it for a while only to lose it and have to start searching again.

He had seen no sign that Big Cat had caught one of the wolves, but he knew that the forest was large and he hadn't searched everywhere.

He finally realized that his only hope was to get to the den and howl to see if he could attract the others. He headed toward the den, afraid of what he might find.

It was fully dark when he got close to the den. Suddenly, he sensed a movement. Something was coming toward him, fast. Before he could react, Sweetbreath crashed into him, knocked him over and began barking and happily licking his muzzle.

Her barking attracted the other two, and soon the four wolves were rolling around like puppies sharing their joy at being back together.

Runt spent a couple of minutes nuzzling Beauty to show her that he was glad she had overcome her fear and helped save the pack.

When Runt realized that he had spent most of the day looking for his packmates who had simply made their own way back to the den as soon as they were clear of Big Cat, he felt foolish. He should have known what they would do. He realized that he still had a lot to learn about being a pack leader.

He wished Big White were here to help him, but Big White was gone. He would have to learn how to be a leader just like every wolf before him — the hard way.

In the meantime, there was only one thing to do. It was time to celebrate.

Runt led his pack to the top of their rocky den area. When they were all assembled he lifted his muzzle and began to howl. It wasn't the sweet, joyous song they had sung to the full moon, but a low, soft song of thanks for being alive and together.

As the sunlight filled the room, Clay began to wake. It was strange because it seemed like he was still in his dream. He could hear the wolves howling. At first, he could hear all four wolves, but then he only heard one, and it was loud.

Clay sat straight up, immediately awake. At the foot of his bed, Gunny's muzzle was pointed toward the sky, and he was howling. It didn't sound like anything Clay had ever heard a dog do before.

A few seconds later his Dad ran into the room, followed soon after by the rest of the family. Grandpa Sam was the last one in, and Gunny stopped howling just as he arrived.

Gunny dropped his head and held it low for a minute. When he raised it, he looked like he had just woken up. He looked around at all the people staring at him as if to say, "What's going on? What are you people doing here?"

"Clay, are you OK?"

"Yeah, Dad, I'm fine. A little confused but fine."

"What the heck was Gunny doing?" Maddie asked.

"He was howling," Sam replied.

"Yeah, I got that, but he didn't sound like any dog I've ever heard."

"No," Rebecca said, "That was his wolf howl."

"His wolf howl?" Mike asked, 'I don't recall you saying anything about a wolf howl before."

"We might not have told you all the details of that search at the Buffalo Wheel," Sam said.

"Yeah, I guess not," Mike replied, "Clay, are you OK?"

"Yeah, but boy do I have a story to tell you."

"What kind of story?"

"The wolves were howling. The Vision was true. I'm gonna find the wolves."

Hannah looked at her son and shook her head, "Clay, if you're making this stuff up …"

"Mom, trust me. There's no way I could be making this stuff up. You'll know what I mean when you hear the whole story."

"Sounds like it's time for another family meeting."

"Sure, Dad, but let's do it after breakfast. I've been in the forest searching for wolves, and I'm starved."

When Clay saw everyone looking at him quizzically, he said, "I'll tell you all about it at the meeting. Let's go eat."

CHAPTER THIRTEEN

Family Meeting II

HANNAH COULDN'T BELIEVE HOW MUCH HER SON ATE for breakfast. Eggs, pancakes, bacon, he kept asking for more. Finally, afraid he would make himself sick, she told him, "No more." Clay looked disappointed for a second, then he jumped up, grabbed a piece of bacon off his sister's plate, and ran out of the room

Maddie suggested that they all go out for some time on the beach before the family meeting, but the girls balked. Maia led the rebellion.

"Please, Mother, we all want to hear Clay's story."

"I think the adults should hear the story first, and then decide if it's something you girls should hear."

"Oh no, Mother. Remember, if it were not for Mara, Iben and I you would not even know that Clay was having these dreams."

"All right, but if I don't like what I'm hearing, I'll send the three of you out of the room."

"Yes, Mother. Of course."

Sam walked into the room and said, "I think we're gonna have to postpone the meeting anyway. Clay's gone."

"Gone? Where?" Hannah asked.

"I went to get him, and he was nowhere around. Then I noticed that Gunny's missing too. I looked outside and saw the two of them about a half mile down the beach."

"Should I go get 'em?" Mike asked.

"No, let 'em go. I don't know what's happening, but Clay evidently feels he needs some time alone with Gunny. They'll be fine. In the meantime, I suggest the rest of us go to the beach."

Twenty minutes later, everyone was on the beach as Clay and Gunny walked back.

"Sorry I was gone so long."

"What were you doing?" Hannah asked.

"I was just tryin' to understand what happened last night."

"You mean your dream?"

"No, I understand that. I'll tell you about it when you're ready. The part I don't understand is at the end of my dream. I was dreaming about the wolves howling, and then Gunny started howling, and it seemed like ... this is gonna sound silly."

"Don't worry," his Mom said, "Tell us what you think."

"It seemed like we were both having the same dream, except I was Wolf Finder and he was one of the wolves. You'll understand when I tell you the whole story."

"Are you ready to do that now?" Sam asked.

"Yeah, I think so."

"This is as good a place as any," Sam said, "Let's pull our beach chairs up together and see what Clay has to say."

" ... so at first I thought it was the wolves calling to me like they had been, but then I realized they were howling, and I could hear them with my ears, not inside my head. I sat up so fast I banged my head on a tree branch, and it really hurt. I mean, you're not supposed to feel pain in a dream, are you?

"Anyway, that woke me up, and I heard the wolves howling, and then it was just one wolf, and then I realized it was Gunny. Then you guys all came in."

"Were you scared, Clay?" his Mom asked.

"At first I was scared because I didn't know if I could do it. I mean Wolf Finder's a kid like me. I think he's the same age. It's pretty scary to be off in the forest on your own with just a spear and a little bow and arrows. Plus I was scared that I'd let The People down. I mean, goin' on a Quest is a pretty big deal, and I didn't know if I could handle it."

"It sounds to me like you did pretty well."

"Thanks, Dad. I was most scared when I first started out. Once I got goin' ... I dunno, ... it's like I was too busy to be scared.

"But here's the really weird thing. This is why I went for my walk. When I think about the dream, I start remembering other things. Things that weren't in my dream but that Wolf Finder did. It's more like I'm remembering something I did instead of dreaming about something some other kid did. Is that anything like the dreams you had Grandpa?"

Sam was quiet for a long time. Then, "Yeah, Clay, I think it is. I didn't try to think too much about those dreams because they were really scary. But when I did think about them, they were more like memories than dreams."

"What do we do now?" Hannah asked.

157

"I don't know that there's much we can do," Sam replied, "We have no control over when or whether he's gonna have another dream, or memory, or whatever. All we can do is listen and help him try to figure out what's goin' on.

"Remember that if this is anything like the dreams we had on Iwo Jima, then Clay isn't in any real danger. The only one who was in danger then was Gunny."

"He may not be in physical danger, but what about emotional danger?" Hannah said. "What if this ends up having some kind of long-term effect on him?"

"Mom, don't worry," Clay said, "I'm not scared. This has been a lot of fun."

"Fun?" Hannah asked. "How can any of this be fun."

"Well, maybe not fun exactly, but exciting. I mean, how many kids get to go on an adventure to find wolves to help their tribe?"

"OK, if you say so. What do you want to do now?"

"Actually, I'm kinda hungry."

"Hungry? After that breakfast you ate? How can you be hungry?"

"Mom, have you ever eaten a marmot? It takes about two hours to kill one, skin it and cook it, and then you don't get much meat off it. When you've been livin' on marmot for a while, you get hungry pretty quick."

Clay looked at his family and realized that they had no idea what he was talking about.

"See? That's what I mean. I didn't dream about eating marmots. It's like something I remember doin'. I bet if I had a marmot or a rabbit, I could make a meal out of it right here. All I'd need is my flint knife and my pouch of fire-making stuff."

"Grandpa, were your dream-memories like that?"

"No," Sam said, "My dreams felt like memories, but I don't have any memories that weren't part of the dream like you seem to have."

"OK, so now what do we do?" Hannah asked.

"I don't know," Sam said, "But maybe you should get Clay in and feed him before he starves."

Hannah looked at Clay, 'You're really hungry?"

"Yes, Ma'am."

"OK, let's go in and see if there's any food left in the house."

Once Clay had finally gotten enough to eat, the rest of the day seemed to go on as usual. The kids played out on the beach, and the adults joined them or sat on the porch reading and talking. Clay told his Mom that he was no longer starving, and he would probably just eat a regular dinner, which he did to everyone's relief.

After dinner, they all sat out on the porch enjoying a beautiful evening. No one was talking until Sam broke the silence.

"What do you think is going to happen tonight, Clay?"

"I don't know. I hope I go looking for the wolves, but it's not something I have any control over."

"You don't remember what you are going to do next?" his Dad asked.

"No, it's like the memories are connected to the dream. After I dream something, then the memory of all the things I didn't dream is just there. Like how to cook a marmot. But I can't, like, predict the future, the stuff I haven't dreamt yet."

Sam looked at Gunny, whose head was swiveling to watch each person talk.

"It looks like he's following our conversation."

"Yeah," Clay said, "I think the same thing is happening to him. He's having dream-memories just like I am, only his are about being a wolf."

"How can you know that, Clay?"

"I don't know it for sure, Dad. That's just the way it seems to me."

Mike turned to his mother, "Mom, next time let's not book our family vacation in the Twilight Zone, OK?"

"Don't blame me," Rebecca said, "Talk to your father and his dog. They're the ones in the middle of all this."

Clay stifled a yawn, "I know it's early, but I'm pretty tired, plus I kinda want to see what happens tonight. Is it OK if I go to bed?"

"Sure, son," Mike said, "See you in the morning."

As Clay left the porch Gunny quickly got up and walked out alongside him.

"What do you think's gonna happen tonight?" Mike asked his Dad.

"I don't know, but nothing bad. There doesn't seem to be any threat in these dreams and Clay seems to be enjoying his adventure. I think all we can do is wait and see what happens."

"There may not be any threat in his dreams," Hannah said, "But eating marmots? They're like weasels, right? Yuck!"

"They're actually more like prairie dogs, and people have been eating things like marmots a lot longer than they've been eating steak," Rebecca said. "It all depends on what you're used to, and it doesn't seem to have bothered Clay."

"No," Maddie said, "He's acting like it's all perfectly normal. What do you three girls think of all this?"

"I think it's really exciting and I can't wait to hear what happens next," Mara said.

Maia and Iben nodded in agreement.

CHAPTER FOURTEEN

Runt and Wolf Finder

GUNNY SLEPT IN CLAY'S BED THAT NIGHT. That was something Gunny rarely did, but when Clay got into bed, Gunny put his front paws up on top of the covers and made a little whine. It took Clay a minute to understand what he wanted, but then he realized that Gunny needed help to get up onto the bed because of his injured back leg. When Gunny was on the bed, he curled up at Clay's feet and almost immediately went to sleep.

As soon as Clay's head was down on his pillow, he heard the wolves howling. The strange, beautiful sound was like a lullaby, and Clay went to sleep and began to dream.

The night was cold, and the fire had gone out, but Wolf Finder didn't notice. He was entranced by the song the wolves were singing. It went on for a minute or two, then stopped. Then one wolf would begin again, always the same wolf. Wolf Finder could tell because each wolf had its own voice. When the leader had sung a few notes, the others joined in one at a time. That's how he knew there were four wolves.

Wolf Finder would have been happy to sit there all night listening, but, eventually, the last note faded away and the wolves went silent. He continued to listen until he began to notice how cold he was. He added some tinder to the embers of his fire and soon had it built up enough to feel its warmth. He wrapped up inside his robe and lay still. He shivered for a few minutes, but his time in the forest had hardened him, and he was soon on the verge of sleep.

His last thought before he drifted off was, *As soon as it is light I will go. Tomorrow I will find the wolves.*

Runt lay awake for a long time after the wolves had finished their song. Again he wished he had Big White and Mother to help him. Big Cat was a danger to the pack, and he had to decide what to do. He knew they couldn't stay here with Big Cat so close, but where should they go?

They had been following the deer toward the place where the sun comes up when they had run into the cat. Did that mean the cat was going in the other direction? There had been no sign of him where they had been before.

What would the deer do? The pack would have to stay near the deer, they needed the food. If Big Cat also followed the deer, what would happen? Would he try to kill the wolves to have all the deer for himself? Runt didn't think so. As powerful as Big Cat was, he was just as vulnerable as the wolves. One bite from the powerful jaws of a wolf in the wrong place could lame him so he couldn't hunt. No, Runt didn't think the cat would fight, but then, how could a wolf know what a cat would do?

He finally fell into an uneasy sleep, but his mind kept working. When he awoke at first light, he had made his decision.

Runt was stretching and yawning as the other wolves came out of the dens. When they all had stretched enough to be fully awake, the others looked at Runt. Runt looked off toward the rising sun and began to trot in that direction.

With only a slight hesitation, Sweetbreath, Clown, and Beauty followed their leader.

Wolf Finder woke before it was light and quickly built up his fire. First Cooker had shown him how to collect seeds from certain grasses that he could mash into a paste with a little water and then heat in his deer stomach. It was a quick way to fill his belly early in the morning, and it could keep him going most of the day.

As soon as he had eaten, he threw some snow on the fire and started off in the direction he had heard the wolves.

Today will be the day that I will finally see a wolf.

As excited as he was, he knew he had to be careful. Just because he wanted to see the wolves didn't mean that the wolves wanted to see him. If these wolves had never seen one of The People before they wouldn't know that he was coming as a friend. He knew that wolves were powerful, dangerous animals. He would have to show them that he was not a threat. First Hunter and First Scout had given him some ideas about how to do this, but no one knew what might work. Once again, he would have to trust the Vision to show him how to act.

He was able to move quickly through the thinning, patchy snow, but he forced himself to go slowly and to look for sign. He hadn't seen anything much larger than a rabbit for days, but he knew that could change quickly. He had not seen any wolf sign, and he hoped that didn't mean that they were moving away from him. He put that thought away and continued to walk with the sun and the wind at his back.

Although the wolves were his main focus, there was always a worry about Big Cat at the back of his mind. First Hunter and First Scout had told him that Big Cat would be the greatest danger he could face. He remembered their words when he asked them what he should do if Big Cat attacked him.

"You know the story of Great Hunter. The one that Memory tells?"

"Yes, First Hunter."

"Great Hunter was First Hunter a long time before I was born. He is the only one of The People to have killed a Big Cat."

"Yes, I know! As the cat was crouching to attack, Great Hunter charged at him and threw his deadly spear which struck Big Cat in the breast, and he died before he could take his next breath."

"Yes, that is how Memory tells the story. Now I must tell you something that only Chief, Wise Mother, First Hunter, and First Scout know."

"What?"

"Not all of Memory's stories are completely true."

"What? But Memories stories are the true stories of The People."

"Yes, and they are mostly true, but some small things are changed to help The People understand and believe the story. The story of

Great Hunter and the Big Cat is one of those. The story is true, Great Hunter did kill a Big Cat, but he didn't do it by throwing his spear."

"How did he do it?"

When First Hunter told him, Wolf Finder understood why the story had been changed. The way that Great Hunter had killed Big Cat was so daring and brave that most of The People would either be frightened or disbelieving if they heard it.

"Is that the only way to kill Big Cat?"

"It is the only way that we know. It is the only way that we can show you. It is also the reason why I told First Toolmaker to make your spear longer than normal."

"Does First Toolmaker know how Great Hunter killed Big Cat?"

"No, but he may have guessed something. He is a good man, he will stay quiet."

Wolf Finder blinked his eyes and shook his head. *I have to stop thinking of the past. Pay attention! Look for sign*!

He forced the thoughts of Big Cat out of his mind and went on his way looking for the wolves.

The weather was warming, and there was less snow every day. In the clearings, there were places where bare ground could be seen. Runt knew that the deer would be getting stronger and harder to hunt. But he also knew that they would soon be giving birth to their young, which would tie them down. He thought that the hunting would still be good for a while yet.

The wolves trotted through the forest moving from side to side following the wind and sniffing for the scent of prey. Now though, they were also alert for the scent of Big Cat. His scent was strong in the area where they had fought him the day before, and they made a wide circle around that place. They didn't see any tracks or get his scent, but they stayed alert.

They also didn't get any scent of deer until after the sun had traveled more than halfway across the sky. A short time after they first got the scent, they crossed the track of a small herd and began to hunt. The deer were still moving toward the place where the sun comes up, just as they had been. When they got close to the deer, Sweetbreath and Beauty started to move away to get upwind of the deer to chase them down toward Runt and Clown.

Runt made a soft *woof,* and when Sweetbreath looked at him, he shook his head. She looked confused for a moment and then understood. Runt didn't want them to split up. Until they knew what Big Cat would do, the pack would stay together. It would be safer, but it would make hunting the deer harder.

As it turned out the hunt wasn't very hard at all. When they got close to the herd, one of the big bucks got their scent, and he sprang away running through the forest with the rest of the herd following him. All except one deer, a young buck, who could hardly walk. When the pack had chased him down and made their kill, they understood what had happened.

The buck had an ugly claw wound in one of his hind legs. It looked like something only Big Cat could do, and with one sniff of the wound, Runt knew that was what had happened.

This discovery only raised more questions in Runt's mind. Big Cat should have been able to quickly kill a deer with this severe an injury.

Why hadn't he? Except for this one deer, they had neither seen or smelled any sign of Big Cat. Where was he?

Runt put these thoughts aside while he and the others fed. When they had finished, he had a decision to make. There was enough meat left on this deer for at least one more good meal. Usually, the wolves would stay near a kill like this to defend it from other predators until they had eaten all they wanted. But what if Big Cat was attracted to their kill? Runt didn't want to fight Big Cat. He needed to know more before he could decide.

With their bellies full, the wolves were content to rest and doze. Runt went to each one and got them on their feet and made them follow him. They were going to scout the area around their kill and see if they could find out what Big Cat was doing.

Wolf Finder was disappointed that he hadn't seen any wolf sign. With the sun sliding down toward the Place Where The Sun Goes At Night he was running out of time. He wanted to keep going, but First Hunter had warned him against going too long without food. "You never know when you may need to run or fight, so always have some food in your belly," he'd said. Wolf Finder found a small clearing that was almost free of snow where he could gather some acorns and other nuts that he could crush and eat quickly.

He was finishing his meal when he felt a trembling in the ground and then heard the sound of many hooves running. He just had time to get behind a tree when a large buck deer ran past him followed by an entire herd. The deer were passing so closely on either side of his tree that he could see the panicked look in their eyes and hear their frantic breathing.

He could have easily put his spear into one of the deer, but he didn't. The deer were running from something, and he hoped that it was the wolves. If it was, then they were close, and he wouldn't have time to kill and butcher a deer. He would wait.

When all the deer had gone past, Wolf Finder stood quietly almost holding his breath. Soon he heard what he was listening for. There was the sound of growling and snarling, and it was only a few spear-throws away. He had never heard this sound before, but he knew what it must be. The wolves had made a kill, and they were feeding.

Now was the time to put into action the plan he had thought of every night since he started his Quest. He must be sure that the wolves would accept him, that he would neither scare them off or make them attack to defend themselves. He had decided the way to do this was not to go to the wolves but to let the wolves come to him. The first thing he needed was something to attract them.

He unslung his bow, notched an arrow, and went in search of a big, fat rabbit.

Luck was with him, and he soon got his rabbit. He thought that this was a good sign. He skinned the animal, gutted it, and saved the guts in a pouch he made from the skin. Then he continued on to where he had heard the wolves.

He was so excited that he would soon be with the wolves that he almost missed the big paw print, but just as he was about to step over it he looked down, and what he saw made the hair on the back of his head stand up.

It was exactly as First Hunter had shown him. The print was as big as both of his hands. There was no doubt that it was Big Cat, and this print wasn't very old. He looked around. About the length of his body away he saw another paw print, but that was all. It was very strange. There were just two prints. How could an animal the size of Big Cat leave only two paw prints behind?

Then he remembered something else First Hunter had told him, and he looked up. Studying the trees carefully, he could see a claw mark here and a broken branch there. Big Cat was traveling through the trees! Wolf Finder realized that he could be in great danger, and he stopped to think.

He paused and gave thanks to the Vision for this warning. Now he knew that he had to watch the trees and the ground and to go slowly so that he wouldn't miss any more sign.

For just a moment he thought about turning back. He could go home and tell The People that he'd never found any sign of wolves, that it must have been a false Vision. He would be safe, and he could live a long life.

But what kind of life? He knew that the Vision was true. He didn't understand why he had been chosen, but he had. If he turned away, he might live a long life, but what kind of life could it be, knowing that he had betrayed the Vision and The People.

No, he would go on. He would go slowly and carefully, but he would find the wolves.

Or die trying.

As the wolves scouted, Runt was happy to see that Beauty was keeping her eyes and nose up checking the trees. Runt took the pack back in the direction from which the deer had come. The herd's track was easy to follow.

Now the breeze was blowing at their back, and they were almost on top of the dead deer before they smelled it. It was just as it had been the day before, except here there was only one deer that had been ripped apart. It was obvious that this was something Big Cat had done. This deer had been almost completely devoured. Why then had Big Cat mauled that other deer? Just because he could?

The wolves found Big Cat's tracks and they were heading away in the opposite direction the deer herd had been going. Runt thought about following to make sure the cat was going away, but with the wind at their back, it would be too easy to walk into a trap. He turned the pack around and headed back toward their kill. They would stay there, for now.

When they got back, it was almost dark, and the wolves got ready for the night. They each dug a shallow hole in a snowbank where they would curl up to sleep. The winter fur of a wolf is so thick and dense that they only needed to be in a den on the coldest nights in the middle of winter. On a spring night like this, their fur would hold in their body heat so well that they wouldn't even melt the snow where they were sleeping.

It was fully dark when suddenly Clown jumped up and began to growl. The other wolves were immediately awake and looking off in the direction of the place where the sun comes up where Clown's nose was pointing.

Runt immediately smelled three odors. One was the smell of the Yellow Beast that ate up the grass and trees and turned them to smoke and blackened stumps. This was odd because he had never smelled the Yellow Beast when there was snow on the ground; snow and water killed the Yellow Beast. The second was the smell of a rabbit that had been eaten by the Yellow Beast. Rabbits that had only been partly eaten by the beast were good to eat.

The third odor was an animal, but it wasn't one that Runt had ever smelled before. He couldn't even tell if it was prey or another predator.

Runt was worried but curious. For some reason, he didn't think that this new animal was a threat. He was a little scared of the Yellow Beast, but he thought there was enough snow that it wouldn't be able to come after him.

The four wolves stood still sniffing and listening. Finally, Runt began to walk toward the place from where the strange smells came. After a few feet, he stopped and looked back over his shoulder. Sweetbreath trotted up next to him, and the two continued to walk. After a long pause, Clown and Beauty followed.

They hadn't gone far when Runt began to see a flickering glow in the trees ahead. This was the Yellow Beast, but it didn't seem to be moving or getting larger as it usually did. This made him even more curious than before. Sweetbreath was beside him, and she seemed to be just as interested as he was. Without looking, he knew that Clown and Beauty were behind him. They were more frightened than he and Sweetbreath, but, after their fight with Big Cat, he knew he could depend on both of them.

Runt and Sweetbreath crept quietly toward the Yellow Beast. As they got closer, they could see that it was in the middle of a small clearing. They could smell the strange animal, but couldn't see it. They thought it must be on the other side of the Yellow Beast.

They came to the edge of the clearing. Runt hesitated, then pushed his head through a low bush in front of him so he could see.

Wolf Finder knew that a hunter must be patient, but he had been waiting so long to find the wolves that it was hard to just sit. He stayed as still as he could, only moving to take a bite of the rabbit spitted on a stick next to the fire.

Then there was movement at the edge of the clearing across from him. He held still, not even turning his head but looking out of the corner of his eye. Two gleaming yellow eyes appeared from behind a bush. A moment later he saw two more. Two wolves, they must be wolves.

Moving very slowly, he reached for the rabbit skin pouch at his side.

Runt didn't know what to make of this new animal. It sat next to the Yellow Beast, and the Yellow Beast didn't try to eat it. Its body was covered in different kinds of fur. Some of it smelled like bison, and some of it smelled like deer. There were places where it had no fur at all.

He glanced at Sweetbreath and saw that she was just as confused as he was. He heard Clown and Beauty a short distance behind.

As Runt watched, the animal slowly rose up and stood on its hind legs and looked at him. Runt had never seen an animal do this before. It was looking at him but not in a challenging way. The animal seemed to be as curious about him as he was about it.

The animal's front paws had no fur on them at all, and it was holding a rabbit hide in them.

And then it did something truly amazing.

Wolf Finder carefully turned his head to look at the wolves. He knew not to stare at them because that would be a challenge. He thought he saw a couple of dark shapes farther back in the trees that might be the other wolves.

Now was the time to see if his plan would work.

Moving as smoothly as he could, he threw the skin pouch full of rabbit guts toward the yellow, gleaming eyes.

Runt's first reaction when he saw the rabbit skin flying toward him was to turn and run, but he made himself stand still. Sweetbreath stood with him.

The rabbit skin landed about half a body length in front of him. His nose immediately told him what was there. Even though he had eaten a short time ago, this was too good to pass up.

He sniffed at the rabbit skin and then looked carefully at the two-legged animal. It didn't seem to be doing anything threatening. He took a step out into the clearing.

For the first time in his life, Wolf Finder looked at a wolf. A real wolf! It was the most wonderful animal he'd ever seen. The wolf came forward slowly until its nose was just above the meat-filled rabbit skin, and then it raised its head and looked into his eyes.

The two animals, the wolf and the boy, looked at each other, and they both had the same thought.

We are different, but we are the same.

Runt lowered his head and ate half the meat in the rabbit skin, and then backed into trees. He wanted to see what Sweetbreath would do.

Sweetbreath looked at Runt and saw that he was calm and relaxed, and she stepped into the clearing.

Wolf Finder thought that the second wolf was even more beautiful than the first. Smaller and not as broad in the chest — a female?

The second wolf also looked into his eyes, and he felt the same connection with her. And then he realized what was happening.

The first wolf ate only half the meat. He shared it with this wolf. Why? Is that what wolves do, or did he want to see what this wolf thinks of me?

The second wolf finished the meat and licked the inside of the skin clean. Then she gave him another long look and backed slowly into the trees.

A second later the two pairs of yellow eyes disappeared. He heard movement back in the trees for a while, and he knew that the four wolves were doing something together, but he didn't know what.

Then, as quietly as the wolves had come, they were gone.

Wolf Finder spent most of the next day hunting rabbits and squirrels. He took his kills back to his clearing. He cooked a rabbit for himself and placed the others around the clearing a little closer to the fire.

That night the same two wolves came into the clearing together. They didn't seem nervous or frightened. They moved around sniffing at the food on the ground and then looking at him. While this was happening, Wolf Finder saw two more pairs of eyes staring at him from the edge of the woods. He tore a piece of meat off the rabbit he was eating and threw it toward the gleaming eyes, which instantly disappeared. A few moments later a wolf stuck his head just far enough out of the trees to get the meat and disappear again.

The first two wolves had each selected a rabbit and settled down to eat. They were only a spear length away. Wolf Finder wanted to go to them, but he knew he must be patient. He threw another piece of meat to the edge of the clearing and watched as the fourth wolf darted out to grab it.

He was excited that he had seen all four wolves and was beginning to establish some trust with them, but he knew that this was just the beginning. It wasn't enough to find the wolves. Somehow he must get them to follow him back to The People. He didn't have a plan for that yet.

Runt ate his rabbit slowly. He wanted some time to learn as much as he could about this Two Leg. He watched everything it did, and his nose was constantly working to sort out all the different smells. Almost everything he saw and smelled was something new and amazing.

Two Leg didn't look strong or fast, but he was a good hunter. He had killed as many rabbits and squirrels as Runt's whole pack could. He also seemed to have tamed the Yellow Beast. It sat obediently in front of him and didn't try to chase him or eat him. It didn't even try to eat his rabbit. Instead, it did something to the rabbit that made the most wonderful smell.

Two Leg saw Runt looking at him and took a piece of the rabbit and tossed it to the ground just in front of him. After a cautious sniff Runt took it in his mouth and chewed.

Delicious!

Two Leg did the same thing for Sweetbreath. When she had eaten it, she looked at Runt. It was clear that she was as curious about this Two Leg as he was.

Runt was closer to the Yellow Beast than he had ever been, and he could feel its warmth. He understood how Two Leg stayed warm even with so little fur on his body. Runt wasn't cold, but the warmth coming from the Yellow Beast felt strangely good.

Runt didn't know why Clown and Beauty were so nervous, but they had always been more cautious than he and Sweetbreath. Runt remembered how frightened Clown had been when they had gone into the forest for the first time.

When Runt had finished his rabbit, he lay still watching Two Leg. Two Leg soon finished his own rabbit and then did another amazing thing. He slowly reached behind him and took a bundle of fur, wrapped it around himself, lay down next to the Yellow Beast, and went to sleep!

What kind of animal would lie down next to the Yellow Beast and surrounded by a pack of wolves?

Wolf Finder knew that he was taking a big chance. He was making himself completely vulnerable to the wolves. He thought that these wolves were wonderful, beautiful animals, but he knew that they were also ruthless killers. What if they just followed their basic instinct and attacked?

Only one way to find out.

He knew he wouldn't actually be able to sleep, but he lay as still and quiet as he could, listening.

As the fire began to die down, he could hear the wolves moving around him. He heard them eating the squirrels that still remained. He could hear the crunching of bones. He could tell that all four wolves were in the clearing with him.

Soon, the sounds of eating stopped, and he could hear the wolves' noses working — sniffing, sniffing. The sounds came closer until two of the wolves were right next to him sniffing along the length of his body. He lay perfectly still and tried to relax.

In a minute it was over. He heard the wolves pad across the clearing, and then they were gone into the forest. He sat up. Except for a faint glow from the embers of his fire, it was completely dark and quiet. He looked up into the sky at all the tiny points of light so far away and gave thanks for his Vision.

This has been the best night of my life.

As the pack trotted through the woods, Runt sorted through his thoughts. When he had sniffed Two Leg, he had gotten many odors, but there was a Two Leg scent, and, having smelled it once, Runt would never forget it.

He was sure that Two Leg was not a threat, but what was he? He was a good hunter and had shared his kill with the pack; something that no other animal had ever done. What did that mean?

As always, Runt thought about what was best for the pack. Could this new animal help them hunt? Were there more animals like this? What would happen if they came upon a pack of Two Legs? Would they all act like this one?

Runt had no answers for these questions. All he could do was wait and see. But he would be careful. He wouldn't do anything to put the pack in danger.

The next morning Wolf Finder was out hunting early. He'd gotten almost no sleep, but he was too excited to stay at his camp. Maybe once he'd hunted, he would rest for a while.

He had already killed or scared away most of the rabbits near his camp, so he was going farther to find his prey. He moved slowly and quietly through the woods looking for rabbits but remembering to keep an eye out for any sign of Big Cat.

Suddenly he had a feeling of being watched. He stopped and slowly turned, and there they were, just about a spear throw away. The wolves were following him. He looked carefully at them and decided that they weren't hunting him, they were just watching to see what he would do.

I guess I'll have to show you how The People hunt.

Runt didn't understand how Two Leg could ever kill a rabbit. He was slow, clumsy, and not very quiet. Runt knew that there was a rabbit not too far away, he could smell it. But Two Leg didn't seem to know the rabbit was there.

A minute later Runt saw that he was right. There was a rabbit right in front of the Two Leg. The rabbit was close, but not close enough to catch. Even a wolf couldn't catch that rabbit, and this Two Leg had no chance.

Then Runt saw that Two Leg was doing something with two sticks in his front paws. He held the two sticks up together, and then they made a noise — *Thwang* — and one of the sticks went flying through the air and went right through the rabbit who dropped to the ground dead!

Two Leg walked to the rabbit and pulled the stick out of its body. Then he took a long, thin stone that grew out of a piece of bone and used it to cut the rabbit open and let its guts spill out on the ground.

The Two Leg then walked a short distance away and sat with his back against a tree.

Wolf Finder watched the four wolves nibbling at the small pile of guts on the ground. It wasn't much of a meal for four wolves, but they were sharing instead of fighting over it. He thought it was just like something The People would do.

This was the first time he got a good look at all four wolves in the daylight. They were four unique individuals, two males and two females, and he was beginning to be able to recognize them by their looks and the way they acted.

Their leader was the boldest. He wasn't the biggest, the other male was larger and looked stronger, but he was the one they followed. He wasn't the best looking of the wolves, his fur was a uniform dark grey with just a little black at his muzzle and ears. What drew Wolf Finder's gaze when he looked at him were his eyes. Yellow with deep, dark centers, they were alive with curiosity and intelligence. All of the wolves were graceful animals who seemed to flow over the ground when they walked or ran, but this one had his own walk, with his head held high and his bright eyes seeming to take in everything around him.

Since The People named all their leaders 'First', like First Hunter and First Scout, he thought of the wolf leader as First Wolf.

His mate was much like him. She was smaller, with fur that was almost the same color, and she looked as intelligent and confident.

Wolf Finder thought that if anything happened to First Wolf, she would be the pack leader.

The second male was a big, strong animal with almost entirely black fur. Wolf Finder knew that this wolf would be an efficient killer on the hunt, but he was less curious and adventurous than First Wolf and his mate. He avoided making eye contact and never came too close. He didn't show any sign of fear, and that was good. A fearful animal is likely to attack to defend itself. Wolf Finder thought he merely lacked the curiosity and confidence of First Wolf and his mate.

The last wolf, the second female, was beautiful. There was no other way to describe her. Her grey, white, and black fur seemed to shine in the sun, and Wolf Finder found it hard not to stare at her. She was the smallest and most timid of the four and never looked directly at him or came too close. Still, she seemed to tolerate him and hadn't shown any sign of fear or aggression.

Wolf Finder was pleased that things had gone so well this far. He had been patient and careful, and he had gotten the wolves to trust him. One wrong move could ruin everything and could even get him killed. He never forgot that these were dangerous animals. But if he was careful, he could get this pack to accept him.

The problem was, he still had no idea how he would be able to lead them back to The People.

When the wolves had finished eating, they stood still in the clearing. Their noses were up in the air searching for scent. The big, black male trotted a few feet forward with his nose working rapidly. The other three pointed their noses in the same direction and began to trot off into the wind.

Wolf Finder scrambled up and began to trot after them with his spear in hand. First Wolf looked back over his shoulder at him, and then turned and focused on the scent he was following.

They're going to let me follow them. I'll be able to watch them hunt.

The wolves began to move faster. It was all Wolf Finder could do to keep them in sight. As he watched, the pack began to form into a line with the two males in the center and the females on either end. They started to run faster.

Wolf Finder had almost lost them when he saw the prey straight in front of him about three spear throws away. It was a single deer, a big buck with a broad spread of antlers. The line of wolves was angling in now, and he understood what they were doing. They were going to try to surround the big buck and cut off any line of escape.

He was surprised that the buck was making no attempt to run.

Maybe I'll have a chance to help.

The buck sensed the wolves coming and lifted his head, but he didn't run. He was a full-grown adult in the prime of his life. He had beaten all the other bucks in the competition for does the past fall, and he believed himself to be the mightiest creature in the forest. He had never seen wolves before, but they were much smaller than him, and he didn't fear them.

Runt was surprised at the size of this deer. He was bigger than any he had ever seen. The wolves had to be careful. If this big deer fought, he could do a lot of damage.

Sweetbreath and Beauty had worked themselves around to the side of the deer and soon would be behind him. They would have it surrounded, but then what? He hoped none of the other wolves did anything rash.

In a minute it was just as he thought. The deer was surrounded, but each time a wolf would try to dart in, the deer would spin and lash out with its great antlers or powerful legs.

Runt had never been in this situation and wasn't sure what to do.

He was about to signal the other wolves to back off when he heard something behind him. He turned his head and saw Two Leg running in his slow and clumsy way with his long stick in his front paw.

Then Two Leg made a loud sound, the first sound Runt had ever heard him make — H a a a y Yah! — and the big stick flew right over Runt's head and buried itself into the chest of the deer!

The buck jumped straight up in the air, came down, tried to run and fell. Runt and the others charged in to make the kill, but they were too late.

Somehow, Two Leg, slow, clumsy Two Leg, had used a stick to kill the biggest deer Runt had ever seen.

This wasn't the biggest buck Wolf Finder had ever seen, but it was close. He was surprised at how easily the deer had gone down. All the time he had spent practicing with First Hunter and First Toolmaker was worth it. The spear had gone right where he'd aimed, right where First Hunter had told him, and the flint spearhead First Toolmaker had put on his spear had easily penetrated the deer's chest and gone to the vital organs.

As he walked up to the deer, the wolves backed away, almost respectfully. He looked at the dead animal and felt a moment of sadness. It was such a magnificent creature. He knew that death was the way of the world and that it came to everything, but it was still sad.

After a couple of quick tugs, he saw that he wouldn't be able to pull his spear out. He would have to cut the animal open to get it, but he would have to do that anyway to get at the meat, so he took his knife out and went to work.

When he had gotten his spear, he stood back to let the wolves feed, but they just looked at him. Then First Wolf lay down, and the others lay down next to him. It took Wolf Finder a minute, but then he understood.

They're waiting for me. They want me to feed first.

He knew that this was something important. It meant that the wolves accepted him as an equal. He would have to handle this carefully.

When The People killed an animal, the hunter who made the kill was given the heart, which he would eat raw. The People believed that by doing this, the hunter would get some of the animal's power, and would become a stronger and better hunter.

Wolf Finder reached into the deer and cut out the heart then held it up for the wolves to see. Then he walked away and sat down next to a tree to eat, leaving the rest of the deer for the wolves.

Runt watched Two Leg carefully. It was amazing how easily the stone that he held in his paw could open the deer up so cleanly. When he pulled out his stick, Runt went to investigate. He sniffed all along it, and it was just a stick. He sniffed the stone on the end, and it was just a stone, but when he licked some of the blood off the stone, it cut his tongue, and he understood how the stick was able to go into the deer.

Runt saw that Two Leg took the heart. That was right. When the pack made a kill, the wolves gave Runt the heart. Runt was a little surprised that Two Leg only took the heart. When the wolves started eating they would eat until their bellies dragged the ground.

Runt was learning that Two Leg was a very different kind of animal.

And, possibly, one that could be very helpful to the pack.

Watching the wolves eat made Wolf Finder glad that he hadn't done anything to make them attack him.

That would be very painful — but not for long.

While they fed, he cleaned up. He went to a nearby snowbank and cleaned the blood off his spear and knife. Then he sat down and sharpened the edges of both. First Hunter had told him, "A good hunter takes care of his tools first, then himself." When his spear and knife were ready, he stripped off his clothes and took a bath in the snow. When he was a Younger, he would hide when his mother wanted to clean him up, but now he found that he liked the feeling of being clean. Sometimes he would take two baths in just one moon-change.

He went back to his tree and sat. When the wolves had finished eating, they gathered around him. First Wolf and his mate lay close, just beyond arm's length. The other two were a little farther away.

The wolves went to sleep, but he sat there watching. He soon noticed that one wolf, the black male was awake. He would raise his head and sniff and look around and put his head down. After he had stood watch for a while, First Wolf's mate lifted her head and sniffed. As soon as she did, the black male put his head down and went to sleep.

All that afternoon Wolf Finder watched the wolves. One was always awake and alert while the others slept. This was just like what The People would do when they were on a hunt. The difference was that the wolves did it without moving or making any noise. When it was time, one wolf woke up and the other went to sleep. Wolf Finder had no idea how they did it, but it made him feel safe.

When the sun was almost down to its sleeping place, he began to get ready for the night. He made a small fire pit and gathered wood. He shaved some kindling from a dry piece of wood and got his fire flint out and began striking it with his stone to make sparks.

Out of the corner of his eye, he could see the wolves watching him intently. When the kindling caught fire, and he started adding small sticks he saw the black wolf and his mate stand up and move a little farther away. First Wolf and his mate stayed where they were.

When the fire was going, he went to the deer and cut off a piece of meat that was larger than he would be able to eat. He wanted to see what the wolves thought of cooked deer.

He hung the meat over the fire so that it would cook slowly, and he turned it every few minutes. At first, the wolves with their bellies full ignored him. Soon though, he saw their noses working as the smell of cooking meat drifted past them. First Wolf stood and came as close to the fire as he dared. His full attention was on the roasting meat. The others soon joined him. Now Wolf Finder was surrounded by wolves.

Wolf Finder slowly cut four long strips of meat and threw one out in front of each wolf who immediately gobbled it down. Then he cut a piece for himself and ate it while the wolves watched. He repeated this until the meat was gone. The wolves had eaten more of his dinner than he had, but he got enough.

When the wolves saw that the meat was gone, they went back to their spots and lay down. Wolf Finder saw that three of them went to sleep and one stayed on watch. Feeling perfectly safe, he rolled up in his robe and went to sleep.

He and the wolves stayed near the deer for one hand of days. After three days, the deer was beginning to smell pretty bad, so Wolf Finder went back to hunting rabbits. The smell didn't seem to bother the wolves who continued to feed.

When The People had more meat than they could eat, First Cooker took it to a cave where he hung it over a smoky fire. This kept the meat from going bad and gave it a flavor that Wolf Finder liked.

When the deer had been eaten, and the bones cracked open for their marrow, it was time to move on. There had been no sign of deer, and they would have to go toward the Place Where the Sun Comes Up to try to find them again.

They left early the next morning. Runt led the way, and he paused and looked over his shoulder to make sure Wolf Finder was with them.

The wolves moved at a steady trot that Wolf Finder was just able to keep up with. He had thought that he was a good runner, but being with the wolves made him feel slow and awkward. By the time the sun was halfway across the sky, the wolves were almost out of sight ahead of him. He picked up his pace to catch up and hoped that he would be able to keep going.

When he got within two spear throws of the pack he heard a sound that made every hair on his body stand erect and stopped him in his tracks. It was a scream but not like any scream he had ever heard. This was the scream of an animal that lived to do only one thing — to kill. He knew that this must be Big Cat.

He saw a blur of golden fur rush in at the wolves, and then he heard another scream, a scream of pain. One of the wolves had been hurt.

He knew that if he stopped to think and make a plan, he might be overcome by fear, so he just ran forward.

When he got near the wolves he saw First Wolf's mate laying still on the ground, her side covered in blood. The other wolves stood around her facing the trees less than a spear-throw away.

There it was, Big Cat. It was larger than he could have imagined, and its huge paws were covered with wolf blood. Its lips were drawn back showing what looked like a mouthful of knives. It had the eyes of a killer, and they were focused on the three wolves still standing. It was crouched, and Wolf Finder could see that it was tensed to spring. It meant to kill the wolves, and he knew it was capable of doing it.

Wolf Finder never slowed.

First Hunter was right. I can't hope to hit that cat with my spear. If I throw my spear and miss, it will kill us all. My only chance, the wolves' only chance, is to do what Great Hunter did.

◆ ◆ ◆

Runt stood between Sweetbreath's body and Big Cat with Clown and Beauty at his side. It was their time to die, but they would die fighting, they would die as wolves.

He had forgotten about Two Leg and was surprised when he ran past and stopped in the open about halfway between him and Big Cat. *What was he doing? He is a great hunter, but he can't kill Big Cat like a deer.*

Big Cat was almost as surprised as Runt, and he paused, but then he uncoiled his great muscles, bounded forward one long stride, and leaped.

Big Cat seemed to float high in the air right toward Two Leg. Runt knew he was doomed.

Then Two Leg did something neither Runt, nor Big Cat expected. He jammed one end of his stick into the ground and pointed the sharp end toward Big Cat.

There was nothing Big Cat could do. When he came down, an instant before he could crush Two Leg's head with his jaws the sharp end of the stick went into his chest. The cat's momentum carried him over Two Leg's head, and he crashed to the ground with the spear deep in his body. The cat screamed again, but this was a scream of pain, anger, and frustration.

Runt and the others were stunned, but Big Cat was still alive. Runt led the other two wolves in the attack, and the fight was over quickly.

Runt sniffed at the cat to make sure he was dead and then went to his mate. He sniffed at her muzzle, and she was still breathing, but the blood was welling up from the wound in her side where Big Cat had raked her with his claws.

Runt stood looking sadly at Sweetbreath. She was dying, and there was nothing he could do.

Wolf Finder lay panting on the ground. Now that it was over, the fear hit him, and he couldn't move. All he wanted to do was lie there and try to forget what had happened.

But something was nagging at him. There was something else he must do.

The wolf! First Wolf's mate. She was hurt.

He scrambled up and ran toward where the three wolves were standing around her. He saw the blood running down her side, and was afraid he was too late. But he had to try.

Remembering what First Cooker had taught him, he quickly cut a large piece of hide from his coat and went to her. Without thinking, he roughly pushed the three wolves out of his way. They were too shocked by what he'd done to react. They just stood, watching and confused.

He pressed the piece of bison hide down on her wound. Then ran off to the nearest snowbank and got handfuls of snow and put those over the hide. Then he knelt down next to her and put his weight down on her.

By the time her bleeding had slowed almost to a stop, his hands were frozen. She was still alive, but just barely.

He remembered what First Cooker had said, "If you are hurt and lose blood, drink blood."

There was plenty of blood around. Using a rabbit skin as a cup, he scooped up blood from the cat and brought it to the wolf. At first, he had to put some on his fingers and let her lick them, but she soon seemed to understand and began to slowly take small licks from the rabbit skin.

Once she was drinking, he went to work on a fire. "If you lose blood, you will get cold, and that can kill you," First Cooker had said, "Stay near a fire." He built the fire as close to the wolf as he could.

When the fire was going, he stopped to think about what to do next. Then he realized that he was being watched. He looked up, and the three wolves were standing, not moving, watching intently.

I hope they know that I'm trying to help.

He took the pouches of dried plants that First Cooker had given him to use if he was tired or sick or in pain. He crumbled half of two of the pouches together and put them in the next cup of blood. He didn't know if wolves got sick like people or if the plants would help if she did, but it was all he had.

There were two other pouches of plants. One was for pain, and one was to stop bleeding. He mixed them together and made a paste. He carefully removed the bison hide and spread the paste over the wounds and then replaced the hide.

When he finished, he was glad to see that the female was still drinking. Maybe there was some hope.

He was surprised to see that the sun was still high in the sky. It seemed like a long time since he had run up and seen Big Cat for the first time. He was glad it was still early. He would have time to get ready for the night.

He would need two things, wood for the fire and food for himself and the wolves. Big Cat was lying there a short distance away, and there was plenty of meat on him, but he had no interest in eating cat meat, and the wolves seemed to think the same. He didn't think the wolves would leave the injured female so he would have to see if he could get some rabbit. Then he would gather firewood.

By the time it was almost dark, he was ready. He had gotten two rabbits. Not a lot of food for three wolves and a growing boy, but enough. There was plenty of wood for the fire. He knew that he would be up most of the night keeping the fire going and giving the female more blood to drink. As it got colder, the blood was congealing so he would have to warm it before he could feed her. He wouldn't get much sleep, but that wasn't important.

When he got down to the last couple of pieces of his rabbit, he decided to try something. He took a bit of cooked meat over to the female and held it in front of her mouth. She sniffed at it for a moment and then raised her head enough to eat it. When she lay her head back down, he put his hand out, and, without thinking about it, reached down and gently ran his fingers through the rich fur on the back of her neck. For a heartbeat he felt the muscles in her back go tense, then she relaxed. As he moved his hand through her fur, he heard and felt a rumbling deep in her chest.

I think she likes this, he thought, *I like it too*.

When he pulled his hand away, she lifted her head and licked it.

When he went back and sat down, he suddenly felt exhausted. *I'll feed her once more and build up the fire. Then get some sleep. When the fire gets low, I'll wake up and feed her again.*

When he was ready, he laid out his mat and robe and settled in. The black wolf and his mate lay down next to the injured wolf on the side away from the fire to protect her and keep her warm. First Wolf lay down next to his mate less than an arm's distance away.

Wolf Finder lay still for a moment, then got up and moved so that when he lay down, he was next to First Wolf. First Wolf looked at him, then rolled on his side so that he was touching both Wolf Finder and his mate.

Warm, and with the scent of wolf in his nose, Wolf Finder went to sleep.

Ever since they had killed Big Cat, Runt had watched Two Leg taking care of Sweetbreath. He didn't understand how Two Leg had been able to stop the blood coming out of her side. Runt was sure that she was going to die, but now she was sleeping peacefully, and there was a chance she might live.

He was worried about some of the things Two Leg was doing. He didn't like seeing Sweetbreath so close to Yellow Beast, and he didn't understand why Two Leg had rubbed his paw through the fur on her neck, but she seemed to like it. Watching the two of them, he almost wished that Two Leg would rub his fur the same way.

He was surprised when Two Leg lay down next to him. Runt didn't think that any other animal had ever done anything like that with a wolf. But, for some reason, it felt right. Without Two Leg, Big Cat would have killed his whole pack.

When Two Leg lay down next to him, he moved just enough so that the two of them were touching. It felt good. He felt safe.

It was almost ten in the morning when Hannah checked on her son for the third or fourth time. Clay was like all teenage boys, he would sleep in late whenever he could, but not at the beach.

When she peered into his room, what she saw was so unusual she went to get the other adults. When they were all outside Clay's room, she motioned to Sam and Rebecca, "Have you ever seen Gunny do this before?"

They looked into Clay's room and saw him and Gunny curled together like they were keeping each other warm on a cold night.

"Nope," Sam said when he'd stepped out of the room, "If we're in a tent on a cold night he'll tuck in close to me but nothing like that. He's never done anything like that when we're indoors."

"Do you think they're OK?" Hannah asked.

"Yeah, they look fine, let's just let 'em sleep and see what Clay can tell us later."

As they were getting ready to leave they heard movement in the room and Clay saying something to Gunny. They all went in quietly and saw Clay raising his head from his pillow.

He looked at them for a moment as if he didn't know who they were or where he was. Then he blinked his eyes a couple of times and said,

"Oh, guys. You're not gonna believe what happened last night."

CHAPTER FIFTEEN

Sees Wolf and Coop

AFTER BREAKFAST, THE FAMILY GATHERED ON THE PORCH. It was a cool, rainy morning, and they wouldn't be going to the beach for a while. Clay had eaten another enormous breakfast while everyone waited anxiously to hear his story.

Knut was the first to speak, "Before Clay tells his story I have some information for everyone. I was able to talk with Doctor Sees Wolf last night, and he was very interested in what I told him about Clay's dreams. He verified everything that Sam and Rebecca told us about the search at the Buffalo Wheel, and, just as Rebecca said, he was happy to tell me about his experience as an Arapaho warrior going off to save, 'a fair maiden,' as he put it. He said it was the most fun he'd had in a long time."

Rebecca smiled and said, "Yes, that's what he told me. I kinda liked the, 'fair maiden,' bit."

Knut smiled and continued, "He also told me that he knows Coop. I should have guessed that. The anthropology and paleontology communities are small and often work together."

"That's interesting," Sam said.

"Yes, he asked if he could share what I told him with Coop, and I said it would be. I hope that's OK."

"Well, the cat's pretty well out of the bag now, so I guess so," Sam said.

"Thank you," Knut said, "Sees Wolf called me just a few minutes ago to tell me that he had spoken to Coop and asked if it would be possible for the two of them to listen in by phone when Clay talks about his dream this morning."

"Mike, Hannah, he's your boy, it's your call," Sam said.

"I'd like to hear what someone outside the family thinks about all this, and I think Coop's a good guy, so it's OK with me," Hannah said.

Mike just nodded.

"OK," Sam said. "Who's got a phone with a good mic and speaker? Let's set it up."

".... so I was lying by the fire with First Wolf next to me, and the next thing I know I'm curled up in bed with Gunny and all you guys came walking in."

"OK," Sam said, "Who wants to talk first?"

"Clay, am I wrong or were you telling that story from two points of view, the boy and the wolf?"

"Yeah, Aunt Maddie, that was weird. It was like sometimes I saw what was happening through Wolf Finder's eyes and sometimes through First Wolf's eyes, except his wolf name is Runt."

"The wolf's name was Runt?" Mara asked.

"Yeah," Clay replied, "And that's weird, too. I know his name and his mate is Sweetbreath, and the other male is Clown and the other female is Beauty, but Wolf Finder doesn't know any of that. When I'm seeing things through Wolf Finder's eyes, I only know what Wolf Finder knows, and when I see things through Runt's eyes, I only know what he knows."

"Sweetbreath? A wolf named Sweetbreath?"

"Yeah, Mara, it's a long story. I'll tell you later."

"Why do you think your dreams have changed? Is this the first time you've seen it like that?" Maddie asked.

"Yeah, it's the first time, and I don't know why. If I had to guess, I'd say it had something to do with Gunny sleeping in the bed with me. He's never done that before."

"Thanks, Maddie," Sam said, "I was going to ask the same question.

"Who else wants to talk?"

"Clay, weren't you scared when you had to fight Big Cat?" Mara asked.

"Sure, but I think I was so worried about the wolves that I didn't really feel scared until it was over, and then I was so busy taking care of First Wolf's mate that I forgot about it."

"Are you scared now?" Maia asked.

Clay thought for a minute, "No, I feel good, like I did something really important."

"I'd like to hear what Sees Wolf and Coop think," Hannah said.

"Why don't you go first, Coop," Sees Wolf said.

"OK, let me think.

"First of all, those are some pretty interesting dreams, Clay. I wish I could have dreams like that.

"I guess I'll comment on Clay's story as a paleontologist. There is nothing that I have heard from Clay that doesn't fit in with what we know, or think we know, about what the world was like fifteen thousand years ago. The way he described the behaviors of the animals and humans is as accurate as any scientific paper I've read. I'll let Sees Wolf comment on Clay's or Oldest Boy's or Wolf Finder's Vision and Vision Quest, but as far as I know, it fits with the little bit we understand about early human religious beliefs.

"One other point. I'm sure we're all wondering if Clay is having these dreams because he and I were talking about the evolution of dogs. I don't think that's the case.

"What Clay and I talked about was mostly the scientific basis for what we believe about how wolves became dogs. I told him a story about what might have happened the first time a human boy met a wolf, but Clay's dreams go far beyond my story in terms of detail, not to mention the inclusion of a cave lion, which is something we didn't even talk about."

"Cave lion?" Clay asked.

"Yep, that's what I'm guessing Big Cat was. The cave lion was pretty much the top predator in Europe back in those days."

"Europe?" Clay said.

"Yeah," Coop replied, "The animals you talked about like the auroch and bison, and Big Cat, sound like the ones living in what is now northern Europe at the end of the last glacial maximum about fifteen thousand years ago. If you had been in North America, Big Cat would have been the saber tooth cat who had big fangs that curved down from its upper jaw and curled below the lower jaw, and you didn't describe anything like that."

"No," Clay replied, "Big Cat had plenty of big teeth, but they didn't curl down out of his mouth."

"Also, the wolves probably would have been different. Most of the wolves in North America at that time were the dire wolf, which was a lot larger than what you described.

"And, of course, since there probably weren't any humans in North America fifteen thousand years ago, I'm pretty sure you were dreaming about a tribe of people living in northern Europe."

"Huh, I guess I never thought about that," Clay said, "There was just the village and the forest, and that was pretty much all I knew about."

"Doctor Sees Wolf, what about you?" Hannah asked.

"First, please just call me Sees Wolf."

"Sure."

"I'm not at all surprised by your son's story for three reasons. First, visions and vision quests are a part of Arapaho culture. I have had many visions myself. Secondly, as you know, my spirit brother is *hooxei*, the wolf. Through my association with him, I believe that I have come to understand wolves better than most people. The actions that Clay ascribes to the wolves he encountered sound perfectly genuine to me. My third reason is Gunny."

"Gunny?" Hannah said.

"Yes. I knew the first time I met him that there was something special about him. I believe that some people and animals live their lives with one foot, or paw, in our world and another in some other world. *Hooxei* is one example, and I think Gunny is another."

"You think Gunny is a spirit, like *hooxei*?" Sam asked.

"No, not exactly. At least not yet. However, I wouldn't be surprised if at some time in the future Gunny doesn't visit you and Clay as a spirit."

"You mean after he's dead?"

"Yes, exactly."

"Do you think that Gunny is influencing Clay's dreams?" Maddie asked, "And, if so, why?"

"Before I answer, let me make a suggestion. I think we would be more accurate if we stop referring to Clay's stories as dreams, and call them what they actually are — memories."

"But how is that possible?" Maddie asked.

"I think it comes back to Gunny. I think that there is a connection between Gunny and First Wolf. Sam, do you remember what I said when you asked if I knew how it was possible for three dogs to turn into wolves when we were up at the Buffalo Wheel?"

"Yeah, you said you thought that the dogs became the wolves they had been fifteen thousand years ago. Are you saying that Gunny was … that he had been …?"

"Yes, I believe that Gunny and First Wolf are one and the same, just separated by fifteen thousand years of evolution. If I'm correct about all this, it might explain why Clay is able to share Gunny's memories of being First Wolf or Runt."

After a long silence, Sees Wolf spoke again, "I can hear that you're having a hard time taking this in, and I understand that it is somewhat outside of modern Western cultural beliefs. But if you were an Arapaho or one of the five-hundred-million Buddhists in the world, it would seem obvious."

"Sees Wolf, what you're saying is the sort of thing that I might expect from an Arapaho medicine man, which you are. But you're also a respected scientist. Do you have a scientific explanation for any of this?" Maddie asked.

"No, this is not the sort of thing that science is very helpful with. Let me tell you my philosophy about science and religion."

"Since the very first days of our species' existence, we have been trying to understand the world around us. As far as I know, we're the only species that does this. For thousands of years that understanding has come to us through religion. Religion can be helpful, but it doesn't teach us how to build computers or send rockets to the moon, for example. Science is great at answering questions about 'how' things work, but it's not very good at answering questions that start with 'why.' It's also not much help in trying to understand things like 'good' and 'evil.'

"I try to use science and religion to answer the questions that they are each best suited for."

"Then you're another example of someone with a foot in two different worlds," Maddie said.

"Yes, I suppose you're right."

"Sees Wolf, Coop thank you. I think it's been good for all of us to get an outsider's view of what's been happening," Sam said, "Does anyone else have any questions or comments?"

Maia and Iben raised their hands.

Sam smiled, "You don't have to raise your hands. What is it, Maia?"

"We only have two more nights left on our vacation. We have to find out what happens to Clay and Gunny, I mean Wolf Finder and First Wolf. Clay must finish remembering!"

"It doesn't work that way, Maia. I don't have any control over my dreams, or memories, or whatever. They just come. I don't even know what the finish might be. Maybe I'm going to have fifteen thousand years of memories."

"That would be a really, really long nap, Clay," Mara said, "You'd better get started."

"Very funny, Mara," Clay replied.

"Maia, Iben, I think we're all anxious to hear what happens next," Sam said, "If we don't get to a finish tonight or tomorrow, we'll be able to get everyone together on FaceTime to talk about whatever happens next after you get home."

"In the meantime," Rebecca said, "It looks like it's starting to clear up. I think we should spend the rest of the day on the beach once the sun comes out."

"Sam, Rebecca, it was good to talk with you again," Sees Wolf said, "I'm just as interested in what happens next as the rest of you. I hope you'll be able to keep me updated."

"Yeah, me too," Coop said.

"Don't worry, guys," Sam said, "We'll keep you in the loop."

CHAPTER SIXTEEN

Going Home

HANNAH AND MADDIE HAD A TALK WITH THE THREE GIRLS. They asked them not to bother Clay with a lot of questions about his memories. Although he was acting like his normal, teenaged-boy self, they didn't think it would be good to put a lot of pressure on him. They promised that the girls would be included in any discussions with Clay.

The weather cleared up right after lunch, and the family went to the beach. The sun was bright, but the air was still pleasantly cool. It didn't take long before all four kids were too busy having fun to worry about what might happen that night.

After a long afternoon on the beach, Sam and Rebecca took the whole family to the Riverview Cafe in Sneads Ferry for their a big seafood dinner. The Riverview wasn't a fancy place, but it sat right at the mouth of the New River where it emptied into the ocean, and most of the food they served had been swimming that morning.

Clay filled up on fried oysters, fried shrimp, french fries, and hush puppies. At his mother's urging, he even managed to eat some cole slaw.

"Clay, I can believe you were a caveman all those years ago," Mara said, "You sure eat like one."

"I gotta stock up, Mara," Clay replied, "I got an injured wolf to take care of and no tellin' what might happen tonight. I'll need my strength."

The six adults just shook their heads.

When they got back to the house, Gunny seemed more happy than usual to see them. As soon as he'd had his potty break outside he stood at the foot of the stairs and looked back at Clay.

"I get the impression Gunny's ready for bed and he wants you to join him," Rebecca said to Clay.

After a big yawn, Clay said, "Yes, Ma'am, I think you're right. You'd think I'd be wide awake after all that sleep I had last night, but I'm really tired. I feel like I actually did all those things I was dreamin' about … or remembering, or whatever."

"OK," his Mom said, "Head on up. Let us know if you need anything."

"Thanks, Mom. G'night everybody."

Clay walked behind Gunny going up the stairs in case he needed some help with his bad leg.

When Clay came back to his room from the bathroom, he found Gunny with his paws up on the bed.

"I guess we're sleepin' together again, huh?"

Gunny just looked at Clay.

"OK, up you go."

Once Gunny was settled, Clay lay down with a groan. *I really do feel like I did all that stuff in my dream. I'm exhausted. I never thought that sleepin' could make you tired.*

With that thought, he fell back into his memories.

◆ ◆ ◆

The next morning everyone was in the kitchen and dining room waiting for Clay. Gunny had already come down, and Sam had taken him out for his potty break, so they knew that Clay was awake. It was a beautiful day outside, but no one wanted to go to the beach until they found out what had happened last night.

Clay stumbled down the stairs a few minutes later looking like he was half asleep.

"Did you have any more memories last night?"

"Oh yeah, Mom. It just keeps getting better. Can I get something to eat before I start talking?"

"You as hungry as you were yesterday?" his Dad asked.

"Yes, Sir."

"OK, here, start with this," Mike said, putting a plate of pancakes and bacon in front of him, "Let me know if you need more."

By the time Clay had finished, everyone was gathered on the porch. Knut had given Sees Wolf and Coop a heads-up, and he would call them when Clay was ready to talk.

When Clay walked out, his mother said, "I don't understand how you can eat so much and not have a swollen belly."

"Wait till you hear my story, Mom, then you'll understand."

"OK, we're all waiting."

"OK, remember the last time I had just killed Big Cat, and First Wolf's mate had been hurt?"

"Yes!" Maia said, "Is she all right?"

"Let me tell my story, and you'll see."

Wolf Finder was exhausted the next morning. He had been up taking care of First Wolf's mate even more than he thought he would be. All of the fear and excitement of the fight with Big Cat had also taken a toll.

As tired as he was, he felt good. The injured female was still alive, and he thought that her bleeding had stopped. He would check on that later. He hoped that he would be able to remember all of the things First Cooker had taught him about taking care of wounds.

For now, his main problem was food, both for himself and the wolf. At first light, the other three wolves had gotten up together and walked off into the forest.

They're going hunting. They'll be back soon. I hope.

While he waited, he looked at the wolf lying next to him.

I have to have some better way of thinking about her and the others. I need to give them names.

The other male will be Black, because of the color of his fur. The other female's name is also easy. She will be Beauty. But what about the leader and this one? What will their names be?

First Wolf is a name for a leader, but he is more than that. He is the wolf I trust the most. He is dependable, and there is something more. I feel something when I see him and when he looks at me. I feel like he is becoming my friend. Last night when we slept side by side, I felt closer to him than to any of The People except my Mother and Father.

The People have a word for someone like that, a best friend.

They are called Dogca. I will call him Dogca.

And this one? What will I call this one?

THE VERY FIRST DOG

As he had been thinking, almost half asleep, he had been unconsciously stroking the wolf's side. He had just begun to feel a slight roundness in her belly when he heard and felt a low rumbling in her chest.

Startled, he sat up and quickly pulled his hand back. The wolf had raised her head and was looking at him. He was afraid that he had angered her, but then she put her head back down and lay there breathing evenly.

He tentatively reached out and touched her side. She didn't move. He slowly began stroking her fur again. Soon he heard the deep rumbling sound again. It was like the sound she had made when he was rubbing her neck last night.

She likes it! She wants me to keep doing it.

As he stroked her belly, he felt the roundness again.

That answers the question of her name. I will call her Mother.

"Wait a minute!" Mara said, "You called your wolf, 'dog'? How could you call your wolf dog when there weren't any dogs back then?"

"First of all, Mara, he's not my wolf. He's a wolf. Wolves don't belong to anyone.

"Secondly, I didn't call him 'dog' it just sounds like that. If you listen carefully, there's a kind of soft 'cuh' sound at the end. And I picked that because that's the word The People use for someone who's their best friend."

"Can I make a comment?" Coop asked.

"Sure," Clay said.

"Thanks. Mara, that was a very good question. One of my interests is historical linguistics, which is the study of how language and words originate. As soon as I heard that Clay had named First Wolf 'Dogca,' I went online to check it out.

"The Oxford English Dictionary is probably the most authoritative source for all things having to do with linguistics. According to the OED, there was an Old English word 'dogca,' spelled d-o-g-c-a. The OED doesn't give a pronunciation, but it could well be the way Clay described it. 'Dogca' became 'dogge,' which became 'dog' the word we use today.

"Now here's the fascinating part. There is no agreement on where the word 'dogca' came from. It may have come from the Latin 'dogca canum', but no one really knows."

"Coop, are you saying that Wolf Finder may have been the first one to use the word 'dog,' or something that sounds like 'dog' as the name for an animal that looks a lot like a dog?" Maddie asked.

"Well, that would be a real stretch, but I guess it's possible. What do you think Sees Wolf?"

Sees Wolf answered immediately, "We're sitting here listening to an American teenage boy tell us about his adventures with a pack of wolves fifteen thousand years ago, and you think it's a stretch to believe that this boy may have been the first to use the word 'dog'? That doesn't even budge my 'Hard-to-Believe Meter.'"

Coop chuckled, "Yeah, Sees Wolf, you're right. If we can believe that Clay, or someone that Clay used to be, killed a seven-hundred-pound cave lion with a spear — and I do believe that — then I guess we shouldn't quibble over what he named his wolf."

"He's not my wolf!" Clay cried in exasperation.

"Maybe not yet," Sees Wolf said, "But I think he soon will be."

"OK, Clay," Sam said, "Go on with your story."

When Runt and the others came back, each carrying a fat rabbit, the first thing he saw was Two Leg rubbing the fur on his mate's chest. Then he heard the rumbling in her chest.

Runt dropped his rabbit and walked up to Two Leg, and they looked straight into each other's eyes. Wolves seldom did this because it could too easily be mistaken for a challenge, but Runt wasn't worried. Somehow, he and Two Leg had come to understand each other.

After what seemed like a long time, Two Leg slowly raised his front paw and held it up where Runt could see. Then, moving even more slowly he placed it on the side of Runt's face and slowly began moving it back and forth.

What happened next was something neither of them expected. Runt lowered his head and took a step forward until he and Two Leg were touching forehead to forehead. Two Leg brought his other paw up, and soon he was rubbing Runt's fur on both sides of his face. Runt closed his eyes, and his body relaxed.

They might have stayed like that for a long time, but Runt heard Sweetbreath make a soft whine, and he turned to check on her.

He sniffed at her wound, and it didn't smell bad. She didn't seem to be in pain.

Maybe she's hungry? That would be a good thing.

Runt looked at Clown who understood immediately what he wanted. Clown began to tear pieces of meat off his rabbit, which he chewed in his mouth to soften. He then gently put a mouthful of meat down in front of Sweetbreath, who sniffed it then immediately gobbled it down.

Runt got his rabbit and brought it to Two Leg and dropped it at his feet. Two Leg cut the rabbit open and dumped the guts on the ground for the wolves. Then he went to work making Yellow Beast bigger and hotter.

Wolf Finder was happy to see Mother eating. That must mean that she was not hurt too badly. When he watched the wolves eat, he realized how hungry he was. He went to work on his fire and soon had the rabbit roasting over the flame.

When he had eaten enough to take the edge off his hunger, he decided to try something. He took a piece of cooked meat and cut it into four slices. He took one slice to Mother and held it in front of her nose. She sniffed once or twice and then, as if it were the most natural thing in the world, gently took it from his fingers and ate it.

He tried the same thing with Dogca who was a little more hesitant, but he too ended up taking the meat, not quite as gently, from his fingers.

Black and Beauty would have none of it. They backed away when he got close. He knew better than to try to force them to do something they didn't want to do, so he threw their slices of meat on the ground in front of them.

When he finished eating, he got ready to take care of Mother. He was anxious to see what her wound looked like. He filled his deer stomach with snow and placed it over the fire. He wanted it hot, but not so hot as to be painful. That's what First Cooker had told him. When his finger told him the water was right, he took it over to Mother and began to pour it over and around the piece of hide covering her wound. It took two stomachs full to get the hide softened enough that he could try to gently pull it off.

When he had the hide off, he tried to examine the wound, but Dogca was there first. He started licking where Big Cat's claws had raked his mate's side. First Cooker had told Wolf Finder to use hot water to clean a wound, but Dogca seemed to be doing a pretty good job on his own. There didn't seem to be a lot of bleeding, just a little bit of blood seeping around the edges.

When Dogca stopped licking for a minute, he got some more hot water ready and poured it over the wound. After he'd done that, he was able to get a good look at the damage Big Cat's claws had done.

There were three parallel slashes across Mother's left shoulder. Big Cat had four claws on each of his huge front paws, so maybe he hadn't gotten a direct hit on Mother. The gashes looked deep, but Wolf Finder couldn't see any bone exposed. Other than that, he didn't know what he should be looking for.

He cupped his hand and poured some water into it for Mother to drink. She lapped it up thirstily. *I'll have to find something I can use for a bowl. She seems to want a lot of water.*

He remembered that First Cooker had told him that cold can help stop bleeding and is also good for pain, so he got several hands full of snow to pack around Mother's shoulder. When he had finished, she gave a big sigh and closed her eyes. Soon she was asleep and breathing normally.

As soon as Mother was asleep, the other wolves lay down around her as they had during the night. Wolf Finder knew that there were many things he needed to do, but he thought a short nap would do him good, and he lay down next to Dogca.

It seemed like only a few minutes later that he felt something cool and wet on his cheek. He opened his eyes, and Dogca's face filled his vision. It was Dogca's nose that he had felt. He sat up slowly and saw that the sun was in the middle of the sky. He had slept much longer than he planned.

When he sat up, Dogca backed off a couple of paces and looked closely at him.

He woke me up for some reason and now I think he wants to make sure I'm awake.

What Dogca wanted was made clear when he turned and headed off into the forest with Black and Beauty.

They're going hunting, and he wanted to make sure I was awake to take care of Mother. That's good. This will give me a chance to get some things done.

The first thing he had to do was to think of all the things he had to do.

Shortly before dark two days later, Wolf Finder leaned back against a tree and surveyed what he'd accomplished. Mother was lying close to the fire at their new camp, which was set in a clearing with a small stream running through it. It was a pleasant spot, and it fulfilled Wolf Finder's two main requirements.

First, there was plenty of water. With more and more snow melting every day he would need a dependable water source while Mother was healing. Secondly, it was far enough away from their last camp that they wouldn't be bothered by Big Cat, who was beginning to smell pretty bad.

The hardest part had been getting Mother here. She was able to stand and sit now, but she couldn't walk any distance. He'd had to make a travois, something he'd never done before. The People used travois all the time to move heavy loads, so he knew what they looked like, but actually putting one together took a lot longer than he thought it would. The wolves were very nervous when he began to drag Mother onto the travois and then to haul her to the new camp, but she'd made no complaint, so the wolves watched him carefully but didn't interfere.

The second hardest thing was getting the hide off Big Cat. He would need some way to prove to The People that he had actually killed this monster. When he'd gotten it off after a half day of cutting and tugging, scraping and cleaning, he found that it weighed more than he did. It would be a long slow trip home dragging this hide behind him on the travois.

That afternoon he had gone hunting with Dogca and Black leaving Beauty to watch over Mother. They found a yearling deer who hadn't yet learned to be wary of wolves coming from downwind. While the two wolves fed, he went back to the camp and got the travois, which he loaded with deer meat and hauled back to camp.

I'm getting a lot of use out of this travois. I should have made one sooner.

With the camp established and with enough food to last them all for a couple of days, it felt good to lean against a tree and relax.

Dogca trotted over and checked on Mother, who seemed to be normally resting. He then came and sat next to Wolf Finder who reached up and began to rub the fur on the back of the big wolf's neck.

This behavior had become almost normal, but then Dogca did something new. He lay down and put his big head in Wolf Finder's lap. Wolf Finder kept rubbing but now moved his hand down to the wolf's throat and chest. The rumbling in Dogca's chest grew louder.

I have chosen his name well. I think this wolf and I will become best friends.

As he sat there half asleep, Wolf Finder wondered at how everything had turned out.

Not only have I made friends with a pack of wolves, but I am sitting here calmly rubbing the fur of their leader. The Vision has been true so far, but the hard part is yet to come. How will I get them to follow me back to The People?

He knew that there would be at least two main problems. The first was Mother. She was going to have young. He didn't know when, but if wolves had their young at the same time of year as most animals, he had less than one moon-change to get them back to The People. That meant that she must be able to move soon. He could wait one hand of days, but no longer. Then they would have to go. The only alternative would be to stay here with the wolves until the young were old enough to travel.

If the wolves would let him.

The other problem, the big problem, was that he still had no idea how he would convince the wolves to follow him. The pack had accepted him as a friend, but would they accept him as a leader? Dogca was their leader. Could a wolf pack have two leaders?

There were so many things he didn't know, but at least he knew what he had to do first. He had to get Mother healthy, and that meant getting her to eat plenty of meat.

Better get started.

Gently moving Dogca's head off his lap, he cut a large piece of deer meat and put it over the fire to cook. There would be plenty for him and some to share. He thought that hand feeding the wolves would be a way to gain more of their trust. Black and Beauty still wouldn't take food from his hand, but they let him get a little closer each day.

When they had all eaten, Mother slowly and painfully got up and limped to the stream to drink. She then walked a short distance away to relieve herself. Then she walked around the camp twice before coming back and easing herself down near the fire.

That's more than she's walked since she was hurt. We may have a chance after all.

When they had all finished eating, he sat down next to the fire. Dogca lay down next to him and put his head back in Wolf Finder's lap.

Runt had been watching Two Leg closely, and the more he watched, the more intrigued he became. Somehow Two Leg had found a way to move Sweetbreath away from that dead cat. Runt thought that they would have to put up with the smell until she was able to walk. Then he had used his stone to take all the fur and skin off the cat. Runt wasn't sure why he did this, but it was something no wolf could ever do.

The most amazing thing was how good it felt when Two Leg rubbed his fur. Wolves were social animals and enjoyed being close to each other, but this was very different. First of all, Two Leg wasn't a wolf, and Runt had never been touched by an animal that wasn't a wolf before. The other strange thing was Two Leg's paws. They weren't like a wolf's paws. They could grab and tug and press, and when Two Leg rubbed with his paws, it felt good. It felt right.

As usual, Runt thought about the good of the pack. He didn't know where Two Leg had come from or where he was going. He did know that if it hadn't been for Two Leg, all of the wolves would be dead or hurt too badly to hunt. He also knew that Two Leg was a good hunter. Slow, clumsy, and loud, but a good hunter. What could he do to keep Two Leg with the pack?

Runt lifted his head and saw that Beauty was awake and on watch. He put his head back down, and, with Two Leg rubbing his fur, drifted off to sleep.

The next few days went by quickly. Wolf Finder was glad to see that Mother was walking a little better each day. He thought that they would be able to leave in two days. If the wolves would follow him.

He went to work getting ready for the journey home. He knew that it had taken more than one hand of days to find the wolves. He wasn't sure how many days exactly. Except for Memory, The People didn't pay too much attention to numbers. He knew that it would be slower going back with Mother being both injured and getting heavier in her belly every day. Also, they would have to find food each day, which would take time. It might take two hands of days or more to get home. He would have to be well prepared.

He learned that it was easier to drag things behind on the travois than to carry them on his back, so he began to pack everything except his spear and bow and arrows on the travois. He cooked all the extra meat they had and wrapped that in a sack he'd made from deer hide. It would give them something on days when the hunting wasn't good.

Since he didn't have very much, it didn't take him long to get ready. Now came the hard part — waiting. He wanted to leave right away, but he had to give Mother as much time to heal as he could.

After they had eaten, Dogca lay down with his head in Wolf Finder's lap. For the first time, Mother lay down on his other side. She used her muzzle to push Dogca's head to the side so she could put her head down in his lap too.

That night the five of them slept together for the first time. Wolf Finder was in the middle with Dogca on one side and Mother on the other. Black was next to Dogca and Beauty next to Mother.

Two days later, Runt sensed that there was something wrong with Two Leg. The first thing he noticed was his scent. He could smell the odor that Two Leg made just before a hunt or when they had been tracking Big Cat. Not exactly a fear smell, but something like a fear smell. Then he saw that Two Leg couldn't sit still. He was moving all the time, doing something, even if there was nothing to do.

Runt knew that something was changing, but he didn't know what it could be. He watched Two Leg even more carefully than usual. When he saw Two Leg put water on Yellow Beast to kill it and then begin to tie himself into the sticks he had used to carry Sweetbreath, he understood.

He's leaving.

By the time Two Leg was ready, all four wolves were sitting together watching.

Two Leg turned and looked at the wolves. Runt thought that he looked worried, and something else. Sad?

Two Leg turned back. Runt heard him take a long, deep breath and begin walking.

Turning his back on the wolves and walking away was the hardest thing he'd ever done. It was harder than fighting Big Cat. He had tried to think of a way to get them to follow him, but there was nothing. They were wolves. They would do what wolves would do, and he knew no way to change that.

What surprised him the most was how much this hurt. These wolves had become more important to him than he'd ever imagined and not just because The People needed them. He needed them. In a short time, they had become a part of him. A part that he felt he was leaving behind.

He wanted to turn and look back to see what they were doing, but he felt that would be wrong. If he was going to lead them, then he must lead. If they didn't follow, then he had failed, and he would miss them for the rest of his life.

Lost in his thoughts, he was startled when four wolves appeared soundlessly alongside him.

They're coming with me! The wolves are coming with me!

The sun was still high when Wolf Finder saw that it was time to stop. Mother was moving slowly and beginning to limp. If they kept going, he was afraid she would be hurt. They found a small pond in a clearing where they could spend the night. As soon as they stopped, he and the two males went to look for food, leaving the two females to rest.

He was beginning to worry a little about Beauty. She had seemed slow and sluggish when they were walking. Almost as slow as Mother. He hoped she hadn't been hurt or gotten sick.

When they came back with enough meat for a small meal, he saw Beauty standing by the pond drinking, and he understood why she was moving so slowly.

She is going to have young also! I haven't been paying as much attention to her as Mother, and I've never touched her, but now I can see how large her belly is. Now I have two mothers to worry about.

When they had all finished eating, he went to the sack of meat he was carrying and got pieces for Mother and Beauty. He would have to make sure they were well fed. He didn't know much about what happened when a female was going to have young, but he knew that

The People made sure that females about to have a baby had plenty to eat.

That night they all lay down together again. He couldn't believe that he was actually sleeping surrounded by wolves. He had never felt safer.

He lay awake for a while because there was one more problem that he had to solve. He wasn't sure exactly where he was, or how to get home.

He had done as First Scout had told him and had left marks on his track as he was looking for the wolves. But since he had found the wolves, they had moved around so much that he'd become a little disoriented. He thought if he walked toward the Place Where the Sun Comes Up but angled a little to his left, he would cross his track. If not, then he would have to angle back the other way, and that could take a long time. Time was something he didn't have much of.

He realized that this was the only plan he could think of and let himself slowly drift off to sleep.

It was two days of slow travel later that he found the first one of his trail marks. He recognized the gnarled, old pine first and then saw the mark he'd made with his knife. Now at least he knew where he was. If he kept moving toward the rising sun, he would be heading toward home.

He found that if he stopped often enough, then Mother and Beauty could go farther each day. Still, it was taking longer than he had hoped, and the two females seemed to be getting bigger all the time. He didn't know what he would do if they stopped following him.

He had no choice but to keep walking.

Five days later Runt was very worried. Sweetbreath and Beauty were moving very slowly, and he thought that they should have denned a long time ago. He felt that they wanted to follow Two Leg as much as he did, but he had to think of what was best for the pack. The puppies were their future. If something happened to the puppies, he didn't think the pack would survive.

He could tell that Two Leg was worried too, but he didn't know if Two Leg understood about the puppies. If Two Leg didn't stop soon, Runt would stop the pack and find dens for the mothers.

Wolf Finder knew they couldn't go on much farther. It was time to find dens for Mother and Beauty. While the wolves rested, he left his travois and went to scout ahead. He wasn't surprised that Dogca followed him.

Two days before, the forest had started to become more open. He thought that meant that they were getting closer to the place where The People lived and hunted, but he wasn't sure.

As he walked, he was continually searching for his trail marks or anything that looked familiar. Then he saw a shape off to his left. An old tree standing high on a rocky hill.

Could it be? Yes! The hill where he'd spent his first night after he'd left home. As soon as he saw it, he knew what he would do.

Runt saw Two Leg jump in the air and make a loud sound that he'd never heard before. Then he started running toward a hill, and Runt followed.

When they got to the top of the hill Runt saw that it was rocky with some small holes or caves that would be good den sites. Two Leg was running around looking in the holes and getting more and more excited.

I hope Two Leg is thinking the same thing I am because I don't think we're going to get Sweetbreath and Beauty past this place.

Yes! This is where I spent my first night and ate the marmot. There are plenty of holes and rock ledges for dens and shelter. The wolves can make their dens here, and I'll make a camp nearby. Then, when the young are old enough, I can take all of them to The People.

Turning to the Dogca, he said, "Let's get the others. Here is where your young will be born. It's safe, and there will be plenty of food. Come. Let's go."

By evening, Wolf Finder and the pack were settled in on the hill. Mother and Beauty had taken no time to choose their dens in small, rocky caves. He had laughed out loud when Dogca had gone to Mother's den and stuck his head inside, and then jumped back out quickly when Mother snarled and snapped at him. The same thing had happened with Black and Beauty. It was clear that the two males were going to have to find their own place to live for a while.

There hadn't been much time for hunting, but he had gotten a couple of marmots and Dogca and Black had each gotten a rabbit in the forest. It would hold them until they could start looking for bigger game.

Wolf Finder was glad to be here and not just for the sake of the females, but because the weather was changing. It had been dry for at least two hands of days, but now he could smell rain on the wind. He'd already found a rock ledge on the opposite side of the hill from the dens that would give him shelter and where he could build a fire. There was enough room for Dogca if he wanted to be with him.

Two days later, Wolf Finder awoke early when Dogca got up suddenly and sat with his ears cocked. It had been raining almost continuously in a slow drizzle since their first night at the den site. Wolf Finder's ears weren't as good as Dogca's, and at first, he heard nothing but the soft patter of rain. Then there was something else, a soft whining and mewing coming from the other side of the hill where Mother's den was.

Dogca started to leave and then stopped and looked back. Since the females had denned, they had not allowed the males close to them. Wolf Finder was the only one who could bring food to them, and even he wasn't allowed too close. Now he could see that Dogca wanted to go check on his mate, but he didn't want to go alone.

Taking a piece of meat from his pouch, he followed Dogca across the top of the hill to Mother's den on the other side. The sound that he'd heard was coming from in there. He didn't want to surprise Mother, so he started talking to her as he slowly walked toward her cave.

"Good morning, Mother. Are those your young that I hear? Are you all right? Would you like some food?"

When he was almost at the den opening, he heard a low growl that told him he'd come close enough. He took the piece of meat and carefully tossed it just inside the den. The growling stopped, and he moved a little closer. Now he could see Mother at the back of the den with some little, wriggling shapes at her side. He couldn't see how many, but he thought it was at least one hand of young. He also saw that Mother wouldn't be able to reach the piece of meat he'd thrown to her, so he very slowly put his hand in, took the meat and tossed it right in front of her. She gobbled it down, and then made a growl that said it was time for him to go away.

Two days later, the same scene was played out at Beauty's den. It looked like she too had a hand or more of young.

It was more than four hands of days later before the first small, furry heads peaked out from their den and saw the world for the first time. Mother and Beauty were very nervous when the little ones met their mates, but it was soon apparent that both Dogca and Black were happy to see these new little wolves and were anxious to begin acting like fathers.

Wolf Finder thought that he should stay away until the young had a chance to get used to these two big males they had just met, but Mother thought differently. She came to get him the first day that all of her little ones were playing outside the dens.

When he sat down near Mother's den, it was the first time he'd seen all of her young together. She had one hand of little ones. It looked like two males and three females, but he couldn't be sure. At first, they cowered behind their mother, but when she and the other wolves sat calmly, they began to venture out to investigate him. One of the males and two of the females came right to him and sniffed all around him while he sat perfectly still. The other two came about halfway, but no closer. He made no move to touch them or do anything that might startle or frighten them. He just wanted to let them get used to having him around.

Later that day, he met Beauty's young. She'd had one hand plus one of young. It looked like three males and three females. This time, two of the males and one female came to sniff him while the others hung back.

That night, his dreams were filled with the images of tiny wolves and the feel of their cool noses and rough tongues on his skin.

While the young had been growing, Wolf Finder had been busy getting food. Each third day or so he would hunt with one of the males while the other stayed back to guard the mothers and young. He and the two males had worked out a way to hunt deer that worked quite well.

They had found three small deer herds less than a half day's walk from the den site. When they needed more meat, they would find one of these herds. The wolf would work his way upwind of the deer and then rush at them to spook them toward Wolf Finder. As the deer ran past his hiding spot, they were too worried about the wolf to pay enough attention to what they might be running into. He almost always had an easy shot to put his spear into one of them.

He always brought his travois along. When the male wolf had eaten, he then butchered the deer and packed the travois with as much meat as he could carry.

The trip back was always slow. He was pulling a heavy travois, and the wolf had just eaten a big meal. Once the young were old enough to begin to eat meat, the trip got even slower.

He was out with Dogca one day, and after they had eaten, he noticed that Dogca was so full of meat his belly was almost dragging the ground. He'd never seen him eat so much before, and he didn't understand why until they got back to the den.

As soon as Dogca got close to the dens, the young ran out to him. They stood on their hind legs to lick at his muzzle. When they did, he would regurgitate some of the meat for each little wolf.

So that's how they feed their young. With warm, partially digested meat. It makes sense.

Some days when he wasn't hunting, he worked on smoking meat. First Cooker had shown him how to do it. He found a small cave where he could hang the meat over a smokey fire. He covered most of the entrance to keep the smoke in. He spent the day tending the fire starting early in the morning before it was light and building the fire up for the last time just before he went to bed. When he wasn't tending the fire, he was gathering wood. It was a lot of work, but when he'd done it three times, he had a good store of meat for when the hunt wasn't successful.

Other days he tended his clothing and tools. His clothes were either in tatters, or too small, or both. His mother had shown him how to use a bone and deer sinew to sew clothes, but his skill was rudimentary at best. When he finished working on his bison hide coat, the result was serviceable but very odd looking. He had outgrown his beautiful deer hide boots and was forced to cut them apart to make simple hide covers for the bottoms of his feet. He was glad that the snow had melted.

His spear point and knife had seen a lot of hard use and needed constant sharpening. He was lucky that neither of them had broken, but he didn't know how much longer they would last.

All in all, he was happy with the way things had gone. He now had a real pack of wolves, but an old worry kept coming back to bother him.

I still don't know if they will follow me back to The People. This is a perfect spot for a wolf pack. Shelter, water, food, everything they need. Why would they want to leave to follow me? If they don't, what do I do? Go home or stay here?

On the day after the mid-summer full moon, Wolf Finder was feeling sorry for himself. He wished that he had been around the fire last night eating food that someone else had hunted and cooked, and talking, actually talking, with other people, and listening to Memory tell her story. He wanted to see his Mother and Father again, and, for the first time, he found himself wondering what Oldest Girl might look like now.

They weren't hunting today, and even though there were many things he should be doing he was relaxing and dozing in the sun propped up against a rock. Two of Mother's young were lying in his lap sleeping. Dogca was watching the other young while Mother rested.

He woke immediately when he heard Dogca's soft growl and saw him staring off into the forest. Something was moving out there. Two or three animals, but they were, … they were, … Yes! They were walking on their hind legs!

First Scout was two paces into the clearing when she heard Dogca's growl and froze. Wolf Finder watched her slowly turn her head to look up at the den site and saw her shocked expression when she saw him sitting there with wolves all around him. He picked up the two young and put them aside and slowly stood.

"Hello, First Scout, it is good to see you again."

"Wolf Finder, is that you?"

"Yes. Stay there. Come no closer. I will come down and talk."

He started down the hill and then stopped and looked back at Dogca. The two looked at each other for a moment, and when he started walking again, Dogca joined him.

When he got close, he saw that there were two other scouts behind First Scout just inside the trees.

"If you will come out and stand quietly next to First Scout, I think that would be best."

When the three people were all standing in the open, he walked up and stopped about three paces away. Dogca was beside him. His hackles were up, but he was calm.

"Hello again. It is good to see you. It is good to see anyone."

"Wolf Finder, we thought you were dead," First Scout said, "You've been gone so long."

"I am fine. I have found the wolves. There are four adults, two male and two female. There are two hands plus one of young. This wolf is Dogca. He is the First Wolf of the pack."

"You have named a wolf as your best friend?"

"Yes. Without him, I would have died long ago."

As Wolf Finder spoke, he reached down and stroked the fur on the top of Dogca's head.

"He allows you to touch him?"

"Yes, he and his mate both. They seem to like it. The other two don't like me to get so close."

"What do you plan to do?"

"I have to stay here until the young are old enough to travel. I think until the moon at the end of summer."

"And then?"

"And then I hope to bring these wolves to The People."

First Scout thought for a moment, "Do you need anything?"

"Some clothes? A knife? A new spearhead?"

First Scout turned and spoke to the others, then said, "We will leave you a good knife and spear, and we will go back home as fast as we can to tell The People what we have found. They will be very happy."

"Thank you, but don't leave right away. Make a camp here, then go hunt. Bring some of the meat and the guts from your kill and leave it near the hill for the wolves. I think it will be good to start to get them used to other people. When you go back, tell First Hunter to send small groups here from time to time with meat for the wolves. Tell him to send different people each time."

"Very well. What about you? Do you have enough to eat?"

Wolf Finder smiled, "I hunt with wolves. I have plenty."

That night, Wolf Finder sat around a fire with the three scouts and got his wishes to eat a meal that had been hunted and cooked by someone else, and to talk with other members of The People.

Except for the fact that everyone was sad because they thought he was dead, the news from home was good. Two of The People had died during the winter, but that was normal. His Mother and Father were still alive and healthy.

First Scout told him that all of The People would be glad to hear that he was alive. "I think Oldest Girl will be particularly happy," she said with a smile.

He told the Scouts his story of finding the wolves and killing Big Cat. He'd had to drag his travois over and show them the cat's hide before they could believe him.

"Wolf Finder, I think you will have a new name when you come home," First Scout said, "You may even be able to choose your own name."

Choosing a name for yourself was a great honor that only a very few of The People received.

"I will be happy with whatever name Chief and Wise Mother choose for me."

That is not entirely true. There is a name I would like to have, but I will wait until I hear what Chief and Wise Mother say.

When he went back to the den site that night, he found Dogca waiting for him. The wolf walked up and lowered his head to be scratched.

I think he's worried about me.

He watched Dogca closely the next day and saw that he didn't relax until the three scouts left to take their news home to The People.

Runt was afraid that Two Leg would leave with the others and was happy when he didn't. If he thought his worries were over then, he was wrong.

Every few days groups of Two Legs would arrive at the den site. They all looked like his Two Leg, but each one had its own scent. Some were male, and some were female, and they all wore different animal hides. They all carried the same kind of sticks that Two Leg used for hunting, and they all seemed to be good hunters.

Most importantly, they shared their meat with the wolves like Two Leg did.

Each time a new group of two legs came, Two Leg would have them make their camp a little closer to the den site. All of the new two legs were frightened of the wolves at first, but when they saw him and Two Leg together, they soon calmed.

Two Leg didn't want the new two legs to go to the den site, but he soon had Runt and the other wolves coming down to the two leg camp. Runt and Sweetbreath would sit next to Two Leg when they all gathered to eat near Yellow Beast. Clown and Beauty would come close, but not too close. The puppies would stay back with them.

Then one night, one of Runt's pups, a little black male who was the most adventuresome of all, trotted straight up to the two legs, sniffed each one, and then went and curled up in Two Leg's lap.

It wasn't long before all of the puppies were coming down the hill to play with the two legs and get pieces of meat that they would take from the two legs' paws.

Runt knew that Clown and Beauty weren't happy about this, but he didn't see any harm. If the two legs wanted to hurt them, they could have used their sharp sticks any time to kill them, but they showed no sign they would do that.

Runt thought that it would be good for the pack to join with the two legs. Wolves and two legs could hunt together and help protect each other from animals like Big Cat.

Besides, it would be nice to be able to lie close to Yellow Beast when it was cold and have Two Leg stroke his fur.

One moon-change later, First Hunter came with three other hunters to the den site.

"Wolf Finder, we have found a small herd of auroch that we have been trying to hunt, but we can never get close enough to them to put a spear into one. Do you think the wolves can help us?"

Wolf Finder thought, "Yes, but not now. We can't leave the young alone. Two wolves must always be with them, and it is too dangerous for only two wolves to hunt something as large as an auroch. But, if you like I can show you how the wolves and I hunt deer."

"Very well."

That afternoon Wolf Finder and the four hunters followed Dogca and Black on the hunt.

"There," Wolf Finder said, "See how their heads just came up and their noses are sniffing? They have the scent of the deer. Now watch."

He made a motion with his hands, and the two wolves disappeared into the trees at a fast lope.

"They are going upwind of the deer," he said.

"And they understand your hand signals?" First Hunter asked.

"Yes, I've taught them some simple signals like 'come to me' or 'stay where you are' that are very helpful when we hunt. I think that only Dogca understands, but the others follow his lead."

"Now, quickly, spread out here and find hiding spots. Soon they will chase the deer down toward us, and we will be able to use our spears."

It happened just as he said and the hunters were able to kill two large deer. They watched in amazement as the two wolves ate until their bellies were bulging and then trotted off.

"What are they doing?" First Hunter asked.

"They are taking food back to the young."

First Hunter thought for a moment, "Ah, yes! I understand. Very smart."

As they walked back to camp with two hunters dragging travois filled with deer meat, First Hunter said, "Do you think you will be able to bring the wolves back with you? I think it will be very helpful to The People to have them hunt with us."

"I think so, but I don't know. I have learned much from Dogca. He is my friend, but he is first of all the pack leader. He will do what he thinks is best for the pack. I hope that he believes as you do that it will be good for the wolves and The People to hunt together, but I have no way of knowing for sure until I try to bring them home with me."

The first leaves were beginning to change color when Wolf Finder decided that it was time to try to bring the wolves home. The young had been born more than five moon-changes before and were now exploring all around the den site and the nearby woods, and making the adult wolves crazy trying to keep track of them all. They hadn't quite gotten complete control of their long, gangly legs, and sometimes they were so clumsy it made him laugh, but he was sure they would be able to make the trip home.

The mothers were ready also. They had been taking turns hunting and now looked much the same as they had when he first saw them.

The bigger question, as before, was what Dogca would do. The lead wolf had a decision to make. The wolves could stay here where they had everything they needed, or they could take a chance, and hope for an even better life with The People. He thought he knew what Dogca would choose.

It was time to find out.

Early one morning when the first chill of the coming cold made their breath visible, Wolf Finder prepared to leave. He made a show of packing his travois and loading a sack with smoked meat. He dragged the travois down the hill, stopped in the clearing, and looked back up at Dogca.

This time there was no hesitation. The four adults walked down the hill with the young gamboling around them. When they were all together, he turned his face toward the rising sun and began to walk.

It wasn't long before they had to stop. The young wolves had thought this was some new game and they had run around playing and chasing squirrels and now they were tired. Having watched their antics before, Wolf Finder wasn't surprised. Although his home was only one day of walking away, he planned on this trip taking two days.

He found a spot where there were some puddles of water where the wolves could drink, and they rested. When they started again, the young were much calmer and content to walk alongside their parents.

That night after they had eaten, all the little wolves curled up as close as they could to their mothers. It was the first time they would spend the night outside their birth den, and Wolf Finder could see that they were more than a little nervous.

Wolf Finder, sleeping in the midst of three hands of wolves, was not nervous at all.

The next day when the sun was just past the middle of the sky, Runt was surprised to find himself walking on ground that had been beaten flat and smooth by the feet of many two legs. He had never smelled so many different scents before.

How many of these two legs are there?

He saw a young female two leg standing in front of them and walked forward next to Two Leg to see her. Two Leg and the female made some sounds to each other, and she stood still for Runt to sniff her. There was a certain odor on her and the same odor on Two Leg.

Are they mates? No, not yet.

The female turned and ran down the packed dirt toward a place where Runt could smell many two legs. He heard a rising volume of two leg sounds. The two legs made a lot of sounds. He hoped they would be quiet soon.

They went a little farther, and Two Leg stopped. He motioned with his paw for Runt to come next to him. Two Leg then motioned for the other wolves to stay where they were.

When they got to where the two legs' den was, Runt stopped in his tracks. He had never seen so many animals of any type together in one place in his life.

These must be the best of hunters to be able to feed so many.

Runt stayed close to Two Leg as they walked toward all the other Two Legs and stopped in front of an old male and female.

"Welcome home Wolf Finder."

"Thank you, Chief. Thank you, Wise Mother. It is good to be home. This is Dogca, the First Wolf of the pack."

"Your best friend?"

"Yes, Chief."

Chief stepped forward and held out his hand for Dogca to sniff.

"Welcome First Wolf. I am Chief. The First of The People."

Wise Mother then stepped forward with her hand out, "And I am Wise Mother. We are glad to see you."

"What do you plan to do now, Wolf Finder?" Chief asked.

"Is that cave where The People killed the bear still empty?"

"Yes."

"I think I should take the wolves there. It is close, but not too close. The People and the wolves can take time to get used to each other."

"That is a good plan," Chief said, "When do you think the wolves will be ready to hunt with us?"

"Soon, before the deep snow."

"That is good, and when will you be ready to tell us your stories?"

Wolf Finder smiled, "Soon also. I am looking forward to telling The People about the wolves."

"And about killing Big Cat?"

He smiled wider, "Yes, that too."

"Wolf Finder, we have talked, and The People have decided that you should be allowed to choose your name."

"Thank you, Chief. I am honored."

"What name would you like? You can be 'Great Hunter.' The People have not had a Great Hunter for many, many moon-changes."

"Thank you, Chief, but I think that I can best help The People by working with the wolves. I would like to be Wolf Master."

"That is a good name. Wolf Master you shall be."

Three days later, Wolf Master brought the wolves to meet all The People for the first time. Some of the wolves, anyway. Dogca and Mother were with him along with three of their young and three of Beauty's young. The others had come halfway with them and would go no farther.

He had sent word to Chief who had told everyone that they were to try to ignore the wolves as much as possible. Let the wolves come to them, don't try to go toward the wolves.

The first few minutes were tense, but when the wolves saw that no one was crowding them or trying to touch them, they began to relax and explore. The young especially. Mother's black male had become the leader of the pack of little wolves, and he led them around the huts and fire pits sniffing and chewing on bits of bone.

Dogca and Mother sat with Wolf Master as he spoke with everyone who came to welcome him home. His Mother and Father were there, looking very proud. Wolf Master was enjoying seeing all his friends and hearing their stories. It had been decided that he would tell the story of his Quest at the next full moon after Memory told her story, so today he was listening.

The small crowd of people around Wolf Master was relaxed and happy until Dogca and Mother suddenly jumped to their feet. A minute later a woman ran up to the group screaming and crying.

"I can't find Sweet Child! I can't find Sweet Child! She is gone. The wolves have taken her!"

Sweet Child was a Different. She was one hand of summers old, but she had not yet learned to speak. She sometimes made sounds, but she had no words. She limped when she walked and couldn't run at all. The People knew that she would never be able to learn a skill that could help The People, but they all loved her and helped to take care of her because she was a sweet child who made everyone who saw her happy.

Wolf Master went quickly to the woman, "Mother, it is all right. No one has Sweet Child. We will all go and help you find her. Where did you see her last?"

"There! Outside our hut. I went inside for just a moment, and when I came out, she was gone! But I saw those little wolves. They were near. I know they have taken her."

"Mother, don't worry. We will find her," Wolf Master said.

Wolf Master motioned to Dogca, and he and Mother fell in alongside him as he walked toward the woman's hut, with the others following.

They were almost at the hut when Wolf Master saw Mother's ears go up and her head turn to the right. Then she turned and started trotting down a trail into the forest with Dogca behind her. Wolf Master began to run to keep up.

"No!" Sweet Child's mother cried, "Not that way. She is afraid of the forest. She wouldn't go there."

Wolf Master ignored her and followed the wolves. He began to hear some strange sounds from just ahead, and he ran faster. He broke into a small clearing and came to a quick stop next to Dogca and his face broke into a big grin.

Soon the entire group was gathered around the clearing laughing and smiling watching Sweet Child rolling on the ground with six young wolves rolling around with her.

These wolves were one-hand-plus-one moon-changes old, and they were no longer small. Each one of them weighed as much as Sweet Child, and they were starting to hunt with their parents, but Wolf Master could see how gentle they were with this little girl.

It's like they know how special she is.

Sweet Child was screaming with laughter. No one had seen her so happy before. She was even saying a word, or at least a sound, they hadn't heard before.

She was saying, "Pup — Pup — Pup."

From that day on, The People called young wolves "Pups."

"….. and that's when I woke up."

"Wolf Master? Another name? Jeez, Clay."

"Sorry, Mara. It's not something I have any control over."

"I liked the story about Sweet Child," Iben said, "That was my favorite part."

"And this poor young girl who could barely walk and couldn't speak came up with the name for young dogs we still use today?"

"Yeah, Grandma, that's how I remember it."

"Is that the end of the story?" Maia asked.

"I don't know. I found the wolves and brought them back to The People, so it's the end of that part of the story, but I don't know if I'm gonna keep remembering or not."

"Clay, you said, 'I found the wolves and brought them home.' Do you think that you and Wolf Finder are one and the same?"

"I don't know, Mom. I know it sounds silly, but that's how it feels when I'm remembering, and I'm Wolf Master now, not Wolf Finder."

"What do you think, Sees Wolf?" Sam asked.

"I don't think it sounds silly at all," Sees Wolf replied, "Nor would William Shakespeare, for that matter."

"Shakespeare?" Maddie said.

"Of course, 'There are more things in Heaven and Earth, Horatio, than are dreamt of in your philosophies,' the three witches, Banquo's ghost, and many other examples."

"What about you, Coop? How does this sound from your perspective?" Rebecca asked.

"If you mean do I think it's possible for a boy to tame a wolf pack in, what, six months or so, then I would say with the right boy and the right wolf, yes, it could be done."

"But this is our last day," Maia said, "We leave tomorrow. I have to know if there is more to the story."

"Maia, it's all right," her mother said, "Clay and Uncle Mike and Aunt Hannah have promised to tell us if anything happens after we leave."

"But it will not be the same!"

"Maia, I'm sorry, but there's nothing I can do," Clay said.

"Oh … all right."

"OK, everyone, one last day at the beach," Rebecca said, "Let's go out and enjoy ourselves, and then it'll be time to start packing up."

The family had a good time together on their last full day. The only thing that was a little odd was that Gunny stayed right next to Clay almost the entire time.

CHAPTER SEVENTEEN

The People and The Wolves

EVERYONE WAS UP EARLY THE NEXT MORNING, but Clay and Gunny were nowhere to be found.

Hannah was just beginning to worry when Mike spotted them on the beach walking back toward the house.

"Where have you guys been?" Mike asked when they came in the door.

"Just for a walk," Clay said, "It's gonna be a while before I see Gunny again, and I wanted to spend some time with him."

"When did you get up?"

"A while ago. Pretty early."

"Did you have any memories last night?"

"Yeah, but I wasn't runnin' around killin' cave lions and stuff, so I feel like I got a good night's sleep."

"Do you feel like talking about it?"

"Sure, let me get some breakfast first."

"Are you starving?"

"Nope. Just a normal breakfast, please."

"OK, but eat quick. I'll let everyone know you've got another story. We're gonna have to work fast 'cause Aunt Maddie and her crew have to catch a plane in Raleigh."

"OK, I can eat and talk if you want."

"No, just eat. I'll get everyone together and ask Knut to get Sees Wolf and Coop on the phone."

All the suitcases were packed and sitting in the living room when everyone got together to hear Clay's story.

"OK, buddy, you've got an hour," Sam said, "Will that be enough?"

"Yeah, I think so. This isn't as long as some of the others."

"OK, go."

"First of all, there's a gap of almost a year between the end of the last story and this one. Don't ask me why, that's just the way it is. I know there's a gap because there are a lot more wolves. There've been two more litters of pups."

"OK," Sam said, "Go on."

"Well, I'm, I mean Wolf Master, is sittin' on a ledge up on the hill where I can see the whole village. He's watchin' Sweet Child play with the new puppies and thinking about what had happened in the last year …."

It was as if Dogca's pack had adopted Sweet Child as one of their own. Sweet Child was the only one that Mother would let close to the new puppies after they were first born, and the wolves always kept a close eye on her. She was having more trouble walking, and when she got tired, she couldn't move at all. When that happened, one of the wolves, either Dogca, Mother, or one of the yearlings from last year's litter would appear as if by magic alongside her. Sweet Child could put her arm around the wolf's neck, — the wolves stood as tall as she did — and the wolf would help her to get home.

It is simple things like that, more than hunting or anything else, that will make The People see what good friends these wolves will be.

As he had expected, the wolves started hunting with The People well before the deep snow. First Hunter had taken the wolves and Wolf Master to hunt the auroch twice and had killed a big cow each time. It had taken almost all of the able-bodied adults of The People to carry home the meat. These two hunts alone would provide nearly enough meat for the winter.

Also as he expected, Dogca's pack had split in half.

Black and Beauty had never become comfortable around people. They were fine on the hunt as long as no one tried to get too close, but they had no interest in living with The People. The puppies also split. Five of them, two males and three females, went with Black and Beauty, and the other three males and three females went with Dogca and Mother.

Dogca and his pack moved in to live with The People. At first, they all stayed near Wolf Master's hut or cave, but as time went on the yearlings began to find their own people. The black male who was the leader of the yearlings paired up with First Hunter; the two leaders seemed drawn to each other. Another male joined First Scout and her family. One of the females found a home with First Cooker, and she quickly became the best fed of all the wolves.

It was interesting how the wolves were changing. They were still wolves. They would hunt together as a pack and in many ways act like wolves. Best of all, they would all gather at the top of the hill from time to time and sing to the moon. The People loved to listen to the wolves sing.

In other ways, they were acting like something different, something new. Their care for Sweet Child was one example. The fact that they would sometimes sleep in a hut or cave was another.

The most significant change was that they seemed to have lost their fear of fire. Dogca and Mother especially liked to get as close to the fire as they could. Wolf Master knew that they didn't need the warmth except on the very coldest night, they just seemed to enjoy being close to the fire.

He knew less about Black's pack. Throughout the winter they had stayed close by in the old bear cave where he had first taken them. Their new pups, six of them, had been born there. Sometimes they would join The People and Dogca's pack on a hunt, at other times they would hunt on their own.

He would go every few days to check on them. When he did, they would tolerate his presence, but not much more than that. They were much happier to see Dogca and Mother, and he was glad to see that the splitting of the pack hadn't affected their friendship.

When he went to see them one day after the midsummer full-moon they were gone. Dogca and Mother sniffed all around and then looked off toward The Place Where the Sun Goes at Night. They raised their muzzles and sniffed the air then sat on their haunches and began a low, mournful howl. When they had finished, they sat quietly and listened.

Wolf Master could barely hear the reply, but Dogca and Mother heard it clearly. When the song had finished, the three of them sat close together.

The old friends had said goodbye.

Mother's new litter of pups, three males and two females, was becoming a problem. Mother had denned in a small cave near where Wolf Master lived with his Mother and Father. As soon as the pups were old enough to leave the den, they had become a subject of fascination for The People. Everyone wanted to see the new pups and play with them and give them food. He was afraid that if this continued, the pups wouldn't learn to hunt properly, so he talked to Chief.

Chief called a meeting with all The People. "You must leave the pups alone and let them grow up normally," he told them, then turned to the smallest person there, "Except for you, Sweet Child. You can play with the pups whenever you want." Then turning back to the others, "Never go to them and pick them up. If they come to you, you may play with them, but only for a short time. And never, ever, feed them! Mother and the other wolves must teach them to hunt, and they cannot do that if the pups are not hungry!"

Another problem was the fact that The People were beginning to call all of the wolves from Dogca's pack dogca, which was confusing, but he didn't know what he could do about it.

Oldest Girl's parents were his third problem. They could see — everyone could see — that Wolf Master and Oldest Girl were well-suited to become mates. They could also see that Wolf Master would one day be one of the leaders of The People, and they wanted him in their family and the sooner, the better.

Wolf Master and Oldest Girl spent a lot of time together, both because they liked being with each other and because Father was teaching Oldest Girl how to be an artist. With all the things that were happening, Father, who was now called First Artist, and Memory were busier than they had ever been recording all the stories and pictures for The People. Wolf Master had spent more than one hand of days with Memory telling her over and over the story of his Quest and the killing of Big Cat. First Artist had used the hide of Big Cat to understand its shape and size and to make many pictures. Now, all The People would know what Big Cat looked like.

Wolf Master knew that he and Oldest Girl would mate, and he was happy about that, but he wasn't in nearly as great a hurry for this to happen as Oldest Girl's parents. He and Oldest Girl talked every day. She enjoyed learning to be an artist and wanted to finish that before she mated and started having young. He was busy helping The People learn how the wolves would fit into their lives. They both wanted to wait.

They just had to convince her parents.

"Clay! You've got a girlfriend!"

"No, Mara. Wolf Master and Oldest Girl are going to be mates. It's not like they're goin' to the movies at the mall every Saturday."

"I think that it is very nice that you have a girlfriend," Maia said.

"What does she look like?" Iben asked.

"Well, she doesn't look like Taylor Swift, I can tell you that."

Coop laughed so hard he almost choked.

"What's so funny, Coop?" Sees Wolf asked.

"It's a long story, I'll tell you later."

"Can I get back to my story now?" Clay asked.

"Clay's got a girlfriend, Clay's got a ...."

"That's enough, Mara. Let your brother finish," Hannah said in her 'or else' voice.

"Yes, Ma'am."

"Go on, Clay."

"Thanks, Mom."

Wolf Master had been so busy getting the wolves settled in with The People that the time since he had come home had gone by quickly. He enjoyed being home, but there was something he missed — being alone in the forest with the wolves.

When he thought back on those days, he remembered the many times that he was frightened or lonely or lost. But he also remembered how good it felt when the wolves accepted him and the pure joy and excitement of hunting with wolves.

He wanted to get some of that excitement back, and there was something he wanted to find out, so he talked to Chief and First Hunter. When he explained what he wanted, they gave him permission to go for one hand of days, no more. First Hunter also gave him permission to take his wolf with him.

When he was ready to leave, he stood at the same place on the trail where he had stood when he embarked on his Quest. This time he wasn't worried or frightened. Dogca and First Hunter's Wolf stood with him. Mother sat a short distance away with her new pups to watch them leave. He began to walk, and the two wolves followed.

Since he had brought the wolves home, The People had spent most of their time hunting in the grasslands that lay toward The Place Where the Sun Comes Up. With the wolves, they could hunt the auroch and the larger deer who lived there. First Hunter and First Scout were even making plans to hunt the giant woolly mammoth if any of them came near enough.

Because of this, The People had not been going very far into the forest. With the wolves, it was easier to hunt in the grasslands. Wolf Master had a hunch about Black and Beauty that he wanted to check.

He had new clothes and new deer hide boots, and it was pleasant walking in the open part of the forest. He knew that the wolves would be alert for any danger so he could let his mind wander and think of his favorite memories from his Quest.

At mid-day, they stopped for a rest, and he shared some smoked meat with the two wolves. He had brought enough meat for a few days because he didn't feel like hunting, but he had his spear and bow and arrows if he needed them.

The forest was quiet and seemed empty. If his hunch was right, that would change soon.

After their rest, they continued walking. The sun was still high enough in the sky to be seen above the trees when he saw the wolves become more alert. Soon, their noses were working testing the air.

They saw the first wolves a little later. He thought he recognized one of the males from Beauty's first litter. They continued to walk, and the other wolves shadowed them. Neither Dogca nor First Hunter's Wolf seemed concerned, so he didn't worry.

The light was beginning to dim when he saw the familiar old tree on top of the hill with wolves sitting at various places on the slopes. As they got closer, Black and Beauty came down the hill and trotted out to meet them. Dogca looked at Wolf Master, and, when he nodded, ran forward to meet them.

After the wolves had sniffed and licked each other's muzzles, he was a little surprised when Black walked right up to him. The big wolf sniffed his hand, gave him a little lick, then lowered his head to be scratched, something he'd never done before. Wolf Master smiled and began to rub the fur on the side of Black's head.

When he finished, he looked around and saw that he was surrounded by wolves; two adults, five yearlings and six pups. These wolves were different, especially the pups. If these had been Dogca's pups, they would have been all over him wanting to play. These pups sat quietly, watching.

Then he realized that these were not the wolves who were different. These were wild wolves, and the only reason that they were not aggressive or defensive was that Black had shown them that Wolf Master and the two wolves with him were not a threat.

Dogca's pack were the wolves who were different, the wolves who had changed.

Maybe it's not so crazy that The People are calling all the wolves 'dogca.'

That night he built a camp in the clearing near the old den site. First Hunter's Wolf stayed with him, but Dogca spent most of the evening with Black. Wolf Master was pleased, and a little relieved, when Dogca came back to spend the night with him.

As he lay in his old ermine robe with Dogca alongside him, he thought about what he'd learned.

Black and Beauty had been smart. With both packs growing, there would soon not be enough prey for all of the wolves plus The People to hunt. They had moved their pack far enough away that they would have their own hunting territory, but they would be close enough that the wolves would be able to mix together from time to time.

This was important. Wolf Master knew that it was not good for a male and a female who were too closely related to mate. The People had very strict rules about this. He thought that the same thing would be true for wolves.

He also thought that not all of Dogca's pups would want to stay with The People. One male and one female from Mother's first litter had gone with Black and Beauty, and three of Beauty's first litter had joined Dogca's pack.

There must be something different about the wolves that stay with The People, something inside them.

That thought made him realize how lucky he had been to find two wolves, Dogca and Mother, who shared that trait. If he had found other wolves, he might have been able to lead them back to The People, but they would not have come into the village to live with them. Or, they might have just killed him, and The People would never know what happened.

He was prepared to spend three nights with Black and Beauty's pack, but Dogca was ready to go home after the second night. The wolves all seemed to get along well, but the only ones that were friendly to each other were Dogca and Black. Even Beauty spent more time with her pups than she did with Dogca. He thought that Dogca and Black must have been together for a longer time than the other wolves and formed a special bond.

I hope I have a friend like that someday.

Black walked side by side with Dogca for a short way when they left and then stopped. The two wolves nuzzled each other for a last time then Black turned to go back to his pack.

Wolf Master, Dogca, and First Hunter's Wolf walked toward home.

It was almost dark when they arrived at the trail leading into the village of The People. Wolf Master could vaguely see that a small group was waiting for them. When they were closer, he saw that it was Oldest Girl and Mother with two yearlings and some of the new pups.

Dogca trotted ahead to Mother, and First Hunter's Wolf veered off to find his master. The other wolves followed Dogca and Mother into the village, and it was just Wolf Master and Oldest Girl.

I am glad to see her. It has been less than three days, and I am surprised at how happy I am to see her.

Wolf Master walked hand in hand with Oldest Girl to find Chief to tell him that he had found the other wolves and to explain why that was a good thing.

That night as he lay sleeping in his old ermine robe Dogca came in and lay down next to him. Mother and Father were sleeping farther back in the cave, and Oldest Girl was sleeping near them. Wolf Master stroked the wolf's head and thought about his life.

So much has happened since I first heard the wolves calling to me. There are more of The People now than there ever were before, and we are well fed, and the babies are fat. We have wolves again! I have a wolf sleeping next to me, my wolf, my Dogca. Soon I will have a mate.

I am happy.

".... And then the dream just faded away, and I went into a normal sleep for the rest of the night. Then, like I told Dad, Gunny and I woke up early to go for a walk on the beach."

"Is that the end, Clay?"

"I dunno, Maia. I think it's the end for now. I think that Wolf Master is getting older faster than I am and maybe I'm not old enough to have grown up memories."

"Huh," Mara said, "What does that mean?"

"Think about it Mara," Coop replied, "Fifteen thousand years ago people seldom lived longer than thirty years. If Wolf Master was Clay's age when the memories started, and two years or so have gone by, then he would be a young adult now, ready to mate and assume a leadership position with his tribe. Clay may have to be a few years older before he's ready for more of Wolf Master's memories."

"But why did he have those memories in the first place?" Hannah asked.

"I doubt we'll ever know for sure," Sees Wolf replied, "But I'm pretty sure this has a lot to do with Gunny."

"The dog with one paw in our world and one paw in some other world," Sam said.

"Exactly," Sees Wolf replied.

"Well I don't know about Gunny," Maddie said, "But both of my feet are in this world, and in this world if we don't get movin' we're gonna miss our flight."

"Right!" Sam said, "Let's get goin'. Everybody give Maddie and her crew a hand getting their stuff loaded then we can take care of the rest of us.

"Sees Wolf, Coop, thanks so much for your help. It was great to get your professional and spiritual insights on all this."

"It was my pleasure," Sees Wolf said, "It was good to talk with you and Rebecca again. It's never dull when you two are around."

"Yeah, well hopefully we'll have some quiet time for a while now," Sam replied.

"Clay, I enjoyed meeting you and talking with you," Coop said. "Please stay in touch."

"Yessir, I will."

"And, by the way, it sounds to me like you've done a pretty good job of answering your own question about where dogs came from."

"I guess so, but I don't think I'd understand it as well without all the stuff you taught me."

"I'm glad I was able to help. So long, pardner."

"G'bye, Coop."

CHAPTER EIGHTEEN

Runt and Gunny

THE PACKING WAS HURRIED, BUT THE GOODBYES WERE SLOW with hugs and a few tears. Everyone agreed that this had been the best family vacation ever, but they said that every time.

Knut, Maddie, Maia, and Iben were the first to go off in their rental car for the four-and-a-half hour drive to the airport in Raleigh. Maia extracted a promise from Clay that he would tell them if he had any more memories. Everyone smiled when Iben gave him a big hug and said, "I love you, Clay."

Mike, Hannah, Clay, and Mara were next. Their drive home to Northern Virginia was longer, but they didn't have to catch a plane. Clay hugged Gunny for a long time and then ran to the car so no one could see that he was crying.

Sam and Rebecca did one last tour around the house to make sure nothing had been left behind and took Gunny for a walk on the beach. Then they loaded up their Subaru wagon and headed south on Highway 17 for a two-day visit with Rebecca's sister near Pawley's Island, South Carolina. After that, they would start their five-day trek back to Utah.

The first half hour or so of their trip was quiet, and then Rebecca asked the question that was on both of their minds.

"So, what do we tell Nan?"

"About Clay and Gunny and Wolf Master and Runt, you mean?"

"Yeah."

"I've been thinking about that. On the one hand, I'd like to keep all this to as small a group as possible, but this is family business, and she's a member of the family, so I think we should tell her."

"Everything?"

"I don't think two days is enough time to tell her everything."

"So, we'll hit the highlights?"

"Yeah, let's try that."

"OK."

Nan lived in one of the many golf communities near Pawley's Island. Her house had a screened porch that looked out onto one of the fairways, and that's where the three of them spent most of their time talking.

Nan was skeptical when Rebecca started talking about Clay's dreams, but the more she heard, the more she believed. Before long, she was asking for more and more detail.

When Sam came back from taking Gunny for his evening walk, the two women were still talking.

"How far have you gotten?" he asked.

"Wolf Finder is just starting his quest," Rebecca replied.

"What do you think so far, Nan?"

"Well, I'm not a hundred percent convinced you guys aren't crazy, but, if nothing else, it's a good story."

"OK if we join you?"

"Sure, have a seat."

Sam sat, and Gunny walked over to a corner of the porch followed warily by Nan's cat, Tweety. Gunny and Tweety had known each other for years but had never managed to get on speaking terms.

As Sam, Rebecca, and Nan talked, Gunny settled into a deep sleep. And began to dream.

Runt was an old wolf now, and no longer the pack leader. His son, First Hunter's wolf, had taken over but had allowed Runt and Sweetbreath to stay with the pack. There had been no reason for them to have to leave. The two legs shared their food with the wolves, and Two Leg made sure that Runt and Sweetbreath were well fed, even when they became too old to hunt.

Clown and Beauty had left their pack when it was their time. Clown had been a good pack leader, and he didn't want the two of them to be a burden when they were too old to hunt. They came to see Runt and Sweetbreath one last time, but Two Leg wouldn't let them leave. He put them in the old bear cave where they'd been when they first came to the place where the two legs lived. Every time the two legs would come back from a hunt they would leave some meat for the two old wolves.

It was this act of kindness and respect that made Runt certain that he had made the right choice when he had brought his pack here to stay with the two legs.

One day last summer Runt and Sweetbreath had gone to see Clown and Beauty. They had found them curled together not moving, not breathing. The two of them lay there with their old friends for a long time remembering all they had done together. Runt was glad that Clown had his mate with him on his final hunt.

Two Leg had found them there. He and some of the two legs had taken their bodies to a nice place in a grove of trees and covered them with rocks so the scavengers wouldn't get them.

Runt knew that his time would come soon. He wasn't sad. He'd had a good life, and he knew that this was the way of the world.

He got up and walked to his favorite spot, a rock ledge where he could look out over the place where the wolves and the two legs lived together. He was glad to see that Sweetbreath was already there. He lay down beside her, and the two of them leaned in together.

Runt could see wolves of all ages; puppies were playing, youngsters were continually moving, exploring with their noses, and older wolves were relaxing. Everywhere he saw wolves he also saw two legs. It was as if his pack and the two legs were now one big pack together.

He saw his Two Leg and his mate with two of their young. The young were playing with some of the puppies. Two Leg sensed that he was watching and raised his paw in greeting to his two wolves.

Runt was relaxed and getting a little sleepy when he noticed that something was changing. His wolves were still there, but now he saw new wolves. Except these animals weren't really wolves. Some of them were bigger than any wolf he'd ever seen. Others were tiny, smaller than a puppy, but they were adults. Some had short fur, and some had long fur. Some had ears that pointed up like a wolf's, but some had long, floppy ears that hung down. There were long-legged wolves who could run as fast as a deer, and short-legged, pudgy wolves who just waddled along. Everywhere he looked he saw these strange wolves.

He glanced at Sweetbreath and knew that she saw the same thing.

As they watched, one of the strange wolves began walking toward them. This wolf was about the size of a small yearling, but the fur on his muzzle was as white as Runt's so he was an old wolf. The rest of his fur was long and gleaming with a color like the sun. His mouth was open, and his lips were relaxed in an easy smile. He walked with a slight limp, and there was a long scar on one hip. He didn't seem worried that he was approaching two large wolves that he didn't know.

Runt and Sweetbreath stood when the strange wolf stopped in front of them to let them sniff him.

His scent was like a wolf scent but different. And there was something else, a very faint odor that Runt couldn't identify, but that Sweetbreath seemed to know immediately. Runt was confused, but then he got it.

This strange wolf has a smell like me! Just a little, but it's there. How can that be?

When the three of them had finished sniffing, Runt and Sweetbreath didn't know what to do next. The new wolf stepped between them, and, as if it were the most natural thing in the world, lay down looking out at all of the strange wolves running around.

After a minute Runt gave Sweetbreath a shrug and lay down alongside the new wolf. Sweetbreath lay down on the other side, and the three of them watched together.

Runt saw something odd. Neither the wolves of his pack or the two legs seemed to see the new wolves. Only the three old wolves lying together like lifelong friends could see them.

Runt tried to understand but realized that he never would. Like a wolf would do, he accepted it. It was pleasant lying here in the sun with Sweetbreath and this new wolf that he felt he had known for a long time.

The three of them drifted off to sleep.

Rebecca had finished talking, and, along with Sam and Nan sat quietly watching Gunny sleep.

"I can't believe how calm and peaceful he is," Nan whispered.

"Yeah, whatever was going on with those dreams doesn't seem to have bothered him," Sam replied.

"I wonder what he's dreaming about now," Rebecca said.

"I doubt we'll ever know. Goodnight, Gunny."

ABOUT THE AUTHOR

Joe Jennings is a search and rescue K9 handler. He and his dog, Gunny (the real Gunny), are certified for live find in both wilderness and avalanches, and human remains recovery on both land and water. They have been on over eighty searches across the Intermountain West. Joe is also a retired U.S. Marine and a veteran of the Vietnam War.

Joe, his wife Betsy, and Gunny live and play in the mountains of northern Utah.

Joe is the author of two other books in the Sam and Gunny K9 Adventure Series, *Ghosts of Iwo Jima* and *Ghosts of the Buffalo Wheel*. Both of these books were selected as finalists for best novel in the Dog Writers Association of America writing contest; *Ghosts of Iwo Jima* in 2017 and *Ghosts of the Buffalo Wheel* in 2018.

AUTHOR Q&A

Q: How accurate or realistic are your descriptions of the evolution of the dog?

A: It has only been recently that scientists have started paying much attention to dogs. After all, dogs are just … dogs. They're everywhere, and there can't be anything very interesting about them. Once we started to understand the critical role that dogs played in our own evolution, they've become more interesting and worthy of study. At the same time as interest in dogs increased, so too did our ability to do DNA analysis of an animal's lineage. Scientists now have a new wealth of data that they are trying to make sense of, and the result has been a number of different theories of how and when dogs evolved from wolves. As Dr. Cooper did in the story, I have selected the theory that seems to make the most sense to me, and I've tried to present that theory accurately. I've done a fair bit of research on this, but I don't have a background in biology, so it may not stand scrutiny by a real expert. If you find something you think I've gotten wrong, see below for my webpage address and let me know about it.

Q. You attribute a lot of human-like attributes to Gunny and the wolves in your story, but dogs have been shown repeatedly to not be self-aware. Do you think anthropomorphizing animals is appropriate?

A. Yes, I think it's entirely appropriate. Let me explain why.

The usual test of whether an animal is self-aware is to see if it recognizes its reflection in a mirror. Human babies do after a certain age, and some apes do. Dogs typically flunk this test. The problem with this is that it's the wrong test. Similar tests done on the dog's primary sensory input, odor, show that a dog recognizes its own odor — much as Runt recognized his scent on Gunny in the last chapter. Dogs, therefore, have a sense of self.

Furthermore, dogs have a theory of the mind. This means that they recognize that other animals have wants and needs similar to theirs and they attempt to figure out what the other animal is thinking. Any dog owner will tell you that their dog is constantly watching them trying to figure out what the human wants the dog to do next. It also seems to me that it would be impossible for dogs or wolves to form and maintain packs without understanding the "other."

If we accept that dogs are self-aware and have a theory of the mind, then we can attribute thought and emotion to them. But what kind of thought and emotion? I have no idea what a dog thinks or feels, so if I'm writing a story that has dogs thinking, the only type of thinking I know how to describe is human. Hence, I anthropomorphize.

That's my story, and I'm stickin' to it, as Sam would say.

Q.: You describe your books as forming an "adventure series," but where's the adventure? Where are the car chases? Where's the towering inferno?

A: The action sequences in my books are based primarily on things I have done or of which I have intimate knowledge. In the real world, things can get pretty exciting without a lot of improbable last-second escapes or computer-generated monsters. I prefer my adventures to be a bit more believable, and I hope that at least a reasonable percentage of you also do.

If you would like to ask more questions or just chat, please visit my webpage at https://ghostsofiwojima.wordpress.com/.

Thanks again for reading.

Made in the USA
Columbia, SC
13 March 2019